CRUEL SAINT

USA TODAY BESTSELLING AUTHOR

T.K. LEIGH

CRUEL SAINT

Published by Carpe Per Diem Publishing, Inc

BOOKS BY T.K. LEIGH

The Inferno Saga
Part One: Spark
Part Two: Smoke
Part Three: Flame
Part Four: Burn

The Possession Duet
Possession
Atonement

The Beautiful Mess Series
A Beautiful Mess
A Tragic Wreck
Gorgeous Chaos

The Deception Duet
Chasing the Dragon
Slaying the Dragon

Beautiful Mess World Standalones
Heart of Light
Heart of Marley
Vanished

CONTEMPORARY ROMANCE

The Dating Games Series

Dating Games

Wicked Games

Mind Games

Dangerous Games

Royal Games

Tangled Games

The Redemption Duet

Commitment

Redemption

The Book Boyfriend Chronicles

The Other Side of Someday

Writing Mr. Right

For more information on any of these titles and upcoming releases, please visit T.K.'s website:

www.tkleighauthor.com

For a free eBook, sign up for T.K.'s newsletter.

To all the romance readers who love their heroes on the morally gray side...

This one's for you.

Content Warning

Some of T.K. Leigh's books may contain content that could be triggering for sensitive readers. For a full list of content warnings for each book and/or series, please visit her website by scanning the code below.

CHAPTER ONE

Gideon

Confucius once said, *"Before you embark on a journey of revenge, dig two graves."*

A wise sentiment, and for most people, probably true.

Revenge was a dangerous business, even under the most noble of reasons. If you hoped to rain vengeance down on another, you'd better be prepared to pay the ultimate price — your life.

But that was the problem with Confucius' warning.

For those of us who had been wronged in such a deplorable, egregious way, we'd already paid the ultimate price.

We were already dead.

At least, *I* was.

I may draw breath. My heart may beat. The neurons in my brain may fire.

For all intents and purposes, I died five years ago.

And now I would make those responsible suffer the same torment I'd endured since that fateful day.

I would have my revenge, even if it was the last thing I did, to hell with Confucius' warnings.

Revenge was why I was here. Why I'd spent the past year of my life becoming someone else. To make them feel my pain. My betrayal.

My anger.

I thought it would get easier as time went by.

After all, I'd survived. Shouldn't I have been content with that? Shouldn't I have found solace in the gift of life when I should have died a hundred times over?

Therein lay the problem.

I no longer viewed life as a gift, but as a cruel curse. Each day was a slow descent into agony as I was left to rot in a hellish purgatory, praying for salvation or damnation.

While I was forced to suffer excruciating pain, they all carried on with their lives, forgetting about me as if I'd never existed.

As if we hadn't made promises to each other, only for her to break them the instant I was gone.

At one point, she was my world. I thought I was hers.

How long did she wait before finding comfort in another man's arms? In my *traitor's* arms?

A year? A month?

A week?

The mere thought of it turned my blood hot, my chest squeezing at how truly insignificant I was. The newspaper I held crinkled in my hands, images of fists and blood flashing before my eyes, as so often happened whenever I thought about the hell I'd endured.

"Are you doing okay? Can I get you any more coffee?"

A cheerful voice yanked me out of my memories, and I snapped my attention to the barista of the coffee shop I'd been coming to every morning since moving to San Diego a few weeks ago.

All because *she* did.

I hadn't approached her yet. Hadn't even been within a few feet of her.

Instead, I'd simply watched her.

After a year of strategizing and scheming their downfall, it all hinged on her. She was the key, my golden ticket to vengeance.

Unfortunately, that came with its own risks. If anyone might figure out who I was beneath the layers of scars marring my body and the new face I wore as a result of several reconstructive surgeries due to even more injuries, it was *her*.

The woman I once dreamed of sharing my life with.

The woman I thought once dreamed of sharing *her* life with me.

Now, she was nothing more than a distant memory, a cruel reminder of everything I'd lost. Everything they'd *stolen* from me.

And now I was going to steal everything from them.

I could just kill them all, as Henry had reminded me time and again, especially if I didn't care what happened to me in the end. I'd gone into this fully prepared to sacrifice myself.

But they deserved to feel my pain. To feel helpless as they lost everything they cared about.

And when they were at their lowest, I'd stare into their eyes as they took their last breath.

No. They didn't deserve a painless death.

They deserved a fucking reckoning.

They acted as my judge, jury, and executioner.

I planned on returning the favor in kind.

An eye for an eye.

A soul for a soul.

"No thanks," I told the barista in a disinterested tone.

"Sure thing." She gracefully glided through the patio area, wiping down the tables, even though it was unnecessary at this early hour. So far, the only other customers had been a few locals grabbing their coffee before heading to work.

"Her name's Ginny," she stated casually as she worked.

"Excuse me?" I snapped my head in her direction, my brows furrowed.

"The girl you watch every morning. Her name's Ginny. Her drink of choice is an Americano with steamed two percent and a stevia sweetener."

I clenched my jaw, fighting against the urge to correct her. Tell her that her *real* name was Imogene.

"Am I that obvious?" I asked, keeping my voice light.

"A little." She shrugged. "Work in a coffee shop long enough and you notice things. Like I noticed you started to come at the same time every morning and sit outside when most people just grab their coffee and rush off."

"I like to watch the sunrise over the ocean." I gestured at the shoreline mere yards away, the waves sweeping onto the sand before being pulled back. Its dark waters reflected a soft orange glow from the rising sun behind the mountains.

"This is California." She narrowed her gaze at me. "The sun *sets* over the ocean. It doesn't rise."

"I still like this time of day before the world wakes up."

"All the more reason you should talk to her. I'm pretty sure she does, too." She nodded into the distance.

I followed her line of sight as a familiar silhouette came into view, the sky a mixture of pinks and blues behind her. Regardless of the early hour, the temperature was already nearing sixty, causing a sheen of sweat to dot her smooth skin. With each of her long strides, her blonde ponytail swung back and forth.

A memory, vivid and painful, played in front of my eyes, stealing my breath.

Running along the beach with her during a weekend trip to Hilton Head. The overwhelming desire to feel every inch of her as soon as we got back to our hotel room. Her pushing me away, claiming she was too sweaty. Picking her up and carrying her into the shower, where we lost ourselves in each other until our skin was pruned and our hunger satisfied.

But not for long.

It never was with us.

I tried to distract myself from the memories by sipping my lukewarm coffee and admiring the view of the California coastline before it became overrun with tourists. But as she grew near, I found it increasingly difficult to keep my attention focused on anything but her.

So much so that when her gaze locked with mine, I couldn't find the strength to look away, even though all reason told me that was exactly what I should do.

Especially when she faltered in her steps, her brows furrowed in confusion.

It was the first time I'd stared into her eyes in five

years. I'd watched her from afar, studied her as if it were my job.

In a way, it was.

But I hadn't allowed myself to get too close for this very reason.

Did she recognize me?

I knew it was a risk, but I convinced myself it was impossible. Even Henry hadn't recognized me when I showed up on his doorstep after having supposedly died four years prior. It wasn't until I told him things about myself that no one else could have known that he realized I was telling the truth. In the aftermath, I endured facial reconstruction surgery, as well as a handful of cosmetic surgeries, all with the added benefit of making my appearance bear little resemblance to the man I once was.

The man who the world thought was still dead.

I held my breath as Imogene's eyes darted over my features, as if trying to place me.

As if wondering if she'd seen a ghost.

A desperate part of me wanted her to recognize me. Wanted her to call out my name. My *real* name, not the persona I'd taken on this past year in order to put my plan into motion.

Her lips parted and she cautiously stepped closer, a question seemingly on the tip of her tongue. But then she shook her head before continuing along the beachfront path, heading toward her townhouse so she could get on with her day.

And her life.

Little did she know, her life was about to be shattered into unrecognizable pieces.

And I was holding the hammer.

CHAPTER TWO

Imogene

The sun warmed my skin as I drove along the La Jolla coast, palm trees gently swaying in the breeze. I'd only been here for a few weeks, but I was already in love with living in Southern California. How could I not be when I was just a couple of blocks from the beach and the weather was always perfect?

At first, I was hesitant about leaving Atlanta. It had been my home all of my life. Hell, I'd even gone to college and graduate school there, too.

But Melanie was right.

It was time for me to leave behind all the bad memories that city held for me and start over somewhere new.

It was a stroke of luck that the women's professional soccer team in San Diego was interested in having me join their athletic training staff. While I'd had offers from a few other professional teams, soccer had always been my passion. To sweeten the pot, one of my closest friends, Melanie, lived just a few hours north in Santa Monica. As reluctant as I'd been to leave Atlanta, I needed this.

Needed a change of scenery.

Needed somewhere I wasn't constantly surrounded by reminders of *him*.

Needed a fresh start.

So far, San Diego gave me precisely that.

I parked my SUV in the driveway and reached for my bag on the passenger seat. As I slung it over my shoulder and made my way along the succulent-lined path to my two-story townhouse, a chill trickled down my spine, awareness causing the tiny hairs all over my body to stand on end. I couldn't shake the feeling I was being watched.

Just like during my run this morning.

My mind flashed back to the man in a dark suit I saw sitting outside The Daily Grind. His silhouette seemed oddly familiar, but I couldn't quite place where I'd seen him before.

It didn't help that I'd had *that* dream again. The one where I heard him calling my name. No matter where I went, how hard I tried, I couldn't find him. When I looked down, my hands were covered with blood.

His blood.

I was fully aware it was just my subconscious playing tricks on me, making me see things that weren't possible. Samuel was gone. At least, that was what my brain reminded me nearly every day for the past five years.

My heart, though... It still didn't get the message.

I wondered if it ever would.

Shaking off the sensation of being watched, I punched my code into the keypad. As soon as I opened my front door, I was assaulted by a rambunctious bundle of white and tan fur jumping on me. The beagle mix's tail wagged frantically as he panted with excitement, showering my face with kisses.

By his reaction, you'd think I was gone eight years instead of only eight hours.

"Down, boy," I ordered, pushing him off me and giving his head a scratch before turning to retrieve a handful of boxes piled on the porch.

With a swift kick, I shut the door behind me and brought today's deliveries into the living area, piling them on top of even more boxes.

I'd only arrived in California a few weeks ago and the chaos of moving still lingered in every room, boxes stacked haphazardly in every available space.

My plan for the weekend was to finally unpack and start making this place feel like home.

"What do you think, Ollie?" I asked my dog. "Should I stop procrastinating?"

His bark was the only response I needed.

"Okay. Okay. I'm sure you hate living in an obstacle course. Don't you?"

Grabbing a knife from the butcher's block, I headed toward today's deliveries. As expected, each one contained items I'd needed for my new home, most of which I already owned but were packed away. Instead of trying to find them, I'd ordered new items of my more important possessions — like wine glasses, a corkscrew, and bath towels.

As I reached the last box, my eyes lit up at the logo of my mother's bakery. While I was content with my decision to leave Atlanta, I missed her. Missed being able to stop by her house and talk to her while we baked together.

I eagerly sliced through the tape on the box, my stomach growling with the promise of having some of her baking.

"Think Grandma baked you some of her pupcakes, too?"

Ollie barked, obediently sitting beside me, his tail wagging when he saw me remove the familiar bakery box from the package it had been shipped in. Swiftly slicing through the twine, I lifted the flap.

But there were no cookies. No cupcakes. No muffins.

A sharp intake of air filled my lungs as I stumbled backwards, the box slipping from my grasp with a deafening crash. A necklace with a heart-shaped pendant skittered onto the hardwood floor, taunting and tormenting me.

Reminding me that I could move thousands of miles away, but I'd never escape my past.

I'd never be free.

CHAPTER THREE

Imogene

This couldn't be happening. Not again. This necklace meant nothing. It was no big deal.

After all, this wasn't the first time I'd received something like this.

Memories of high school and college came flooding back, a constant stream of cruel jokes and taunts about my father, the notorious serial killer.

Asshole teenagers would leave jewelry on my chair in class or outside my dorm room, mimicking his sick signature of taking jewelry from his victims and giving it to my mother.

I was always an easy target for their amusement, especially when a copycat emerged mere years after his arrest, who also took jewelry from his victims and sent it to my mother.

All packaged in boxes from her bakery.

Just thinking about that hellish time suffocated me with anxiety, my stomach twisting into painful knots. My world spun around me, and I placed my hand on the kitchen island. The cool marble only intensified the burning inside, my chest tightening as I fought for air against the onslaught of memories assaulting me like a sadistic movie.

How the copycat eventually helped my father escape prison.

How he abducted me as a way to punish my mother.

How I saw the worst of humanity during those few horrible days.

Bile rose in my throat and I stumbled into the bathroom, retching up the contents of my stomach.

At just fourteen years old, I was forced to experience things I would have given anything to forget.

But I never would.

No matter how much time had passed, witnessing the man whose DNA ran through me rape, torture, and brutally kill several innocent women would never be erased.

The guilt for not doing enough to stop him would never be erased.

Believe me, I'd tried.

It didn't matter how many times my therapists reminded me I did what I had to in order to survive. That if I'd tried to intervene, he would have only hurt those women even worse.

I still felt like I should have done more.

It was one of the reasons Melanie and I became such good friends. She'd been through something similar, having been abducted when she was a little girl by someone hoping to get revenge against her father, who owned a private military firm. She was forced to witness horrific things. Saw the worst in humanity. Spent days wondering if she'd soon be one of the victims she saw her captors kill, as if their lives didn't matter.

When there was nothing left in my stomach, I flushed the toilet and slowly rose to my feet. Ollie nudged my hand with his nose, his dark, concerned eyes staring at me.

"I'm fine, buddy."

He nuzzled me, and a sense of comfort washed over me, despite the memories he held, considering he'd been Samuel's dog.

After his death, we both struggled to cope with the loss. In a way, we helped each other heal.

I gave Ollie's head another scratch, then rinsed my mouth and splashed water onto my face. Taking several calming breaths, I reminded myself that my sorry excuse for a sperm donor was gone. He couldn't hurt me anymore.

The necklace didn't mean anything. It was probably just some asshole with too much free time on his hands playing a prank on me.

That was all I *wanted* to believe it was.

But what if it was more than that?

An unexpected knock ripped through my townhouse, sending a renewed shock of adrenaline through me as Ollie took off and barked at the door. I mentally cursed myself for not installing my camera doorbell yet.

Still on edge, I padded into the hallway and opened the closet, entering my code into the small safe. The door beeped, and I stared at the gun inside as a memory rushed forward.

Receiving a necklace at my apartment in Atlanta.

Samuel witnessing the anxiety that plagued me.

Him dragging me to the nearest shooting range and teaching me how to handle a gun.

Him also teaching me various self-defense moves so I could protect myself.

He'd told me he wanted to know I was safe when he wasn't around.

At the time, I'd gone along, if for no other reason than to spend more time with him.

I never could have anticipated he would soon be taken from me.

Shaking off the memories, I grabbed the pistol and creeped closer to the door.

When a familiar voice echoed from the other side, I came to an abrupt stop.

"Gin. Open up. It's me."

"Liam?" I blinked repeatedly, relief filling me.

That did nothing to sway Ollie's determination. If anything, hearing Liam's voice made him even more upset, his barking shifting into a growl.

"Ollie, hush," I ordered, and the dog obeyed, albeit somewhat grudgingly.

I returned my gun to the safe, then rushed back to the door. As my hand touched the cold metal of the knob, I remembered the necklace. Not wanting Liam to worry unnecessarily, I hastily grabbed the piece along with its accompanying box and shoved it into the depths of my closet before hurrying to the door and flinging it open.

"Liam," I exhaled as my eyes fell on my friend's suit-clad physique. "What are you doing here?"

His dark gaze locked on mine. "You finish your first week at your dream job and you don't think I'd come here to celebrate? What kind of friend would I be?"

He wrapped his arms around me, pressing a tender kiss to my cheek.

As surprised as I was to see him here, I couldn't deny I was comforted by his presence, especially after receiving that necklace. Even so, I couldn't help but feel like I was being watched as I stood in the doorway.

Pulling out of his hug, I scanned the street, searching for anything out of the ordinary. An older man walked his dog along the sidewalk. A young girl rode her pink bicycle, her pigtails swaying with her movements. And a Jeep Wrangler cruised by, surfboards strapped to its roof. All typical sights in this beachside community.

Yet something seemed off.

"You mean to tell me you flew all the way out here just to celebrate me finishing a week of work?" I ushered Liam inside, hushing Ollie's growling once more. The instant I closed the door behind us, I felt better.

Safer.

Liam always had that effect on me.

Years ago, I never could have imagined we'd be this close.

Hell, I never could have imagined he'd respond to my email in the first place.

As part of my therapy, I reached out to the families of my father's victims. It was a daunting task, but I wanted to find closure and make amends, even if I bore no fault for his actions. Hell, when he'd first started killing women, I'd been a child. I still felt the need to do something, though.

Liam was only ten when my father targeted his mother. I wasn't sure what I'd hoped to get out of contacting him. I certainly didn't expect to find the person who would become one of the most important people in my life.

"What are friends for?" He flashed me his debonair smile, but it wavered, betraying his true feelings.

While Liam and I had been friends for a decade now, he'd made it clear that he'd give anything to be more than friends. But I'd always resisted, not wanting to jeopardize our friendship.

Liam was the reason I fought my attraction to Samuel as hard as I did. Samuel was his closest friend. He didn't want anything to come between them.

Like me.

But that only lasted for so long before neither one of us could deny the connection we'd felt from the second our eyes met, despite the nine-year age difference between us.

Regardless, I could see how much Samuel struggled with lying to Liam. We both did. It was why we kept our relationship a secret as long as we did. Not only was Liam his closest friend, but he was also his business partner, the two of them having developed an online gaming platform that combined social media and gaming, allowing users to design and build their own games for others to play.

It was the first of its kind, and many said it would

never gain traction, not with all the other options available.

They were wrong.

It made them both more money than they ever dreamed possible and was now played by over half the population of American children and teens every year.

I just wished Samuel had been around to see all the success.

"I *do* have my own plane, so it wasn't too much of a hassle," Liam's voice pulled me out of my memories. "Plus, I was up in San Francisco for a few meetings and figured I'd swing by and surprise you."

Liam swept his eyes over my townhouse, his mouth turning into a frown at the sparse furniture and stacks of unpacked boxes.

I'd managed to assemble a coffee table and a few barstools for the kitchen island. Other than that, there wasn't much furniture, besides the couch I'd had delivered earlier in the week. Everything I'd bought was still in boxes, including my bed frame. For the time being, I'd been sleeping on my mattress.

"I like what you've done with the place." His tone dripped with sarcasm.

"I'm still moving in."

I poked him in the ribs, then headed into the kitchen and poured some kibble into Ollie's bowl, hoping that would distract him from growling at Liam. He never really liked him. Probably because he sensed Liam had never been much of an animal person.

"I haven't had time to put together all the furniture I bought."

He sighed, running his hands down my arms as I approached him once more. "I told you, Gin. You could just stay at my place. No need to buy furniture that comes in a box."

"And *I* told *you*," I stepped out of his hold. "I wanted to be on the beach."

"You can see the beach from my place. Plus, there are five incredible bedrooms. A pool. Not to mention full-time staff."

While I'd been surprised to learn he'd bought a luxurious home north of San Diego after I informed him I'd taken a job out here, he insisted he'd been looking into buying a place on the west coast since Melanie moved to Santa Monica a few years ago. My move here just solidified his decision.

"I don't need a full-time staff. My contract with the team is only eighteen months."

"All the more reason you should have just moved into my place."

I parted my lips, but hesitated, not wanting to tell him the real reason I didn't want to move in with him, despite how convenient it would have been.

It was bad enough I'd sought comfort in his bed a few

times in the past when the pain of Samuel's loss hit particularly hard, something I immediately regretted afterwards. I didn't want to lead Liam on any more than I already had. Wanted to ensure the lines of our friendship were clear, despite it all.

"It's important for me to do this on my own. To make my own way. Plus, have you seen how close I am to the beach? I can be on my surfboard within ten minutes of waking up in the morning."

"My little surfer girl." He expelled a sigh and brushed a soft kiss on my forehead. "Where is everything?"

"What are you talking about?"

"All this furniture you need to assemble." He slid off his tailored jacket and loosened his tie, draping both of them over a barstool.

He barely resembled the twenty-something graduate student studying computer science who wore cargo shorts and t-shirts practically every day, even in colder temperatures. There was a time he hated the mere idea of wearing suits.

Now, at only thirty-seven, he was one of the youngest self-made billionaires in the country and wore suits daily.

"Out in the garage." I hitched my thumb in the general direction. "But—"

"Then let's get working." He unbuttoned the top few buttons of his shirt and rolled up his sleeves.

"You don't have to, Liam. I'm planning to put a dent in it this weekend." I bit my bottom lip. "Or at least on Sunday, since I need to be at the field tomorrow for the game. Although, I'm not sure how much I'll get done since Melanie's dragging me to the opening of some club tomorrow night. Still, I'm sure I—"

"What? You think you'll be able to assemble a townhouse full of furniture in a few hours on a Sunday by yourself?"

"Melanie's staying over Saturday night. She said she'd help before she had to head back up to Santa Monica."

Liam barked out a laugh. "I've seen the two of you attempt to assemble furniture. It was a disaster. If I leave you and Melanie to do it, I have a feeling I'll be getting a phone call telling me either one or both of you ended up in the hospital."

"You *seriously* want to spend your Friday night helping me assemble furniture?"

"No. I'd rather spend my Friday night just hanging out with you. But since you're stubborn and refuse to move into my place, I have no choice but to spend tonight helping you."

"Thanks, Liam." I gave him a quick peck on the cheek. "It'll be nice to finally have a bed."

He narrowed his eyes on me. "Please tell me you haven't been sleeping on a mattress since you got here."

"I've been busy." I shrugged again, ignoring his frustration.

He dug his long fingers through his sandy blond hair. "You're infuriating. You know that, right?"

"So you remind me whenever you don't get your way," I sang sweetly.

On a long sigh, he pushed the sleeves of his shirt up even more, toeing out of his designer shoes. "Well, better crack open some wine, Gin. I have a feeling it's going to be a long night." His expression fell. "Unless you don't have any wine, either."

Rolling my eyes, I walked into the kitchen and snatched a bottle off the counter.

"That I *do* have."

CHAPTER FOUR

Gideon

The ocean breeze wrapped around me as I sat at my usual table outside of The Daily Grind early on Saturday morning. With each sip of my robust coffee, I watched the waves cresting in the distance, my gaze focused on one body in particular as she bobbed up and down.

Most of the world was still dark, only a small sliver of light peeking over the mountains in the east, casting a golden glow over the tranquil scene.

There was once a time when the break of dawn filled me with dread about what horrors I'd soon face, despite the fact I'd survived another day I wasn't sure I deserved.

These days, however, I looked forward to getting up

early and sitting outside of The Daily Grind with my crossword puzzle as I watched Imogene either run along the beach or bob up and down on her surfboard, waiting for the perfect wave, a sense of calm about her.

It made me wonder what she was thinking about.

Was she thinking about me?

I shouldn't have cared. It wouldn't change anything. Wouldn't change my plan to use her, then toss her aside, just as she had done to me.

Since she'd looked my way yesterday morning and our eyes locked for the first time in years, I hadn't been able to shake the brief interaction. There was something in her expression I hadn't anticipated.

Pain.

Anguish.

Heartache.

I tried to convince myself it was nothing. Even if she didn't pull the trigger, her betrayal was just as bad.

But as she sat astride her surfboard this morning, I felt the same grief. She wore it on every inch of her.

How was I just noticing it now after watching her daily for the past several months?

As the ocean swelled and rolled in the distance, Imogene's body tensed in anticipation. With effortless grace, she hopped onto her board. It brought back memories of the first time I saw her surf during one of our secret trips to Hawaii. There was something so hypnotic about watching her steady herself on her board, not showing a single ounce of fear over the prospect of wiping out. It was that fearlessness that had captivated me from the moment we met.

If she decided not to do something, it wasn't because she was scared. It was because she didn't want to do it.

The same held true today as she rode the cresting wave, her slender body moving with the water.

As she reached the shore, she unhooked her tether and jogged up the sand toward her bag. Droplets of water fell from her body, glistening in the glow of the rising sun. Pulling a towel from her bag, she dried her hair before stripping out of her wet suit.

My coffee nearly slipped from my hand as I watched her, mesmerized by her movements.

I knew I shouldn't stare, but I couldn't look away even if an earthquake rattled the coastline. Her bikini-clad frame was a sight to behold, even from the side view I had. The rising sun played across her curves, high-lighting every inch of the body I once knew so intimately.

After tugging on a pair of yoga pants and a loose t-shirt, she shoved her wet suit into her bag and slung it over her shoulder, carrying her board up the sand.

In my direction.

I quickly shifted my gaze, not wanting her to realize I'd been ogling her. Instead, my sole focus was on my crossword puzzle. Despite my best efforts, I couldn't comprehend a single clue, no matter how many times I read them. My full attention was on the electric current in the air, getting stronger with every step Imogene took toward me, my body responding to her like a magnet drawn to its perfect match.

Much like we were all those years ago.

It took every ounce of resolve I possessed not to look up and drink her in. As she passed the coffee shop, I felt her eyes on me, heating my skin. Then she stopped abruptly and set her board down in the sand.

"Excuse me."

I didn't immediately respond, the sound of her voice stirring up memories I thought I'd buried deep inside me.

It was as sweet as I remembered, the soft Georgia drawl just as endearing as it was the first time I'd met her. Images of my old life flashed in front of me — all the times we'd lie in bed, limbs tangled, her body wrapped tightly around mine as we basked in the afterglow of making love and planned our future.

There was so much we hoped to do. Build a house on a lake. Have kids. Be one of those couples who couldn't keep their hands off each other, even when we were old and gray.

In a heartbeat, that all disappeared.

Suppressing the memories, I forced myself to meet her eyes. My heart pounded in my chest when she sucked in a sharp breath, something akin to recognition crossing her features.

Please let it be because of yesterday.

Please don't let her recognize me. Samuel Tate.

I was no longer him, though.

The man I'd become was nothing like Samuel Tate.

For one, I was now a killer.

And I had every intention of killing again.

A strained silence surrounded us as she raked her gaze down my body. Unlike yesterday, I was dressed casually — a pair of sweatpants and a hoodie with a base-ball hat — giving off the impression I'd just rolled out of bed for my morning caffeine fix.

Now that she was mere inches away, I regretted this decision. Did my more casual attire spark a memory in the recesses of her mind?

I didn't see how that would make a difference when my face barely resembled the man I once was. Should I have worn colored contacts like Henry recommended?

"Can I help you?" I asked, praying she didn't recognize my voice.

I'd purposefully lost my own Southern drawl, and there was an edge to my tone that hadn't been there in my former life. I hoped it was enough.

"I'm sorry." She blinked repeatedly, as if shaking off whatever she was thinking. "Do you mind watching my board for a minute while I duck inside?" She hitched her thumb toward the familiar board.

"Of course." My answer was clipped, disinterested.

Not holding her gaze longer than necessary, I returned my attention to my newspaper, running my pen along the crossword clue.

"Thanks."

Once she disappeared inside, I exhaled a long breath, mentally berating myself to get my shit together. This was what I'd spent the last several months preparing for. I refused to allow my plan to fall apart because of her. I knew being close to her again would be difficult. Would throw me off. Henry warned me as much when he questioned using her in the first place.

Like I explained, she was the easiest way in. Liam and the others weren't as trusting. Not like Imogene had always been.

I planned to use that trust to my advantage.

I just needed to get my head back in the game. Remember why I was doing this. Why I was here.

"Bear in mind."

I snapped my head up, meeting Imogene's eyes again. "What was that?"

She leaned toward me and pointed at the crossword clue I'd absentmindedly underlined. "Ten across. Consider an imaginary animal," she read out loud. "Bear in mind."

I counted the boxes. When it fit, an unexpected chuckle escaped my throat. It felt foreign. When was the last time I'd laughed? Probably five years ago.

"Impressive."

I shouldn't have been surprised. She always had an uncanny ability to make sense out of the most obscure crossword clues.

"I love crossword puzzles." A nostalgic gleam filled her eyes. "I used to do them every morning with..." She trailed off, the breeze blowing her hair in front of her face as she stared into the distance for a moment before clearing her throat. "Well, thanks for watching my stuff."

She spun from me, balancing the tray containing two coffee cups in one hand while she attempted to pick up her board with the other.

"Let me help you with that." I scrambled to my feet, taking the tray from her so she could wrangle her board.

As she did, her shirt rode up, revealing a sliver of skin by her hipbone. My eyes were glued to a familiar symbol in black ink, the sight of it stealing my breath. It was a design I knew too well, three interconnected loops and a spiral, almost resembling the shape of a butterfly's wings.

A memory rushed back, barreling into me with the speed of an avalanche, causing my heart to stutter and race in my chest.

"What are you doing?" Imogene murmured, her voice raspy from sleep.

"Touching you," I crooned, peppering soft kisses along her shoulder blades.

"That's not what I'm talking about. The pattern you're tracing… What is it?"

"The symbol of unconditional love."

She sighed, her body relaxing into mine, as if the reminder of the connection we shared was all she needed.

It was all I needed.

"Because no matter what happens in the future, no matter where we are, I will always love you."

"And I'll always love you." She grabbed my hand in hers, pulling my arms tighter around her. Then she rolled onto her back, meeting my eyes. *"Can I see?"*

"What do you mean?"

With a mischievous glint in her eyes, she leaned over the side of the bed and grabbed a black marker out of the nightstand drawer.

"I want to see." She handed it to me.

I arched a brow. "You want me to…mark you?"

She ran her fingers through my disheveled, dark hair. The feel of her nails digging into my scalp caused my erection to harden against her once more. It didn't matter it had only been mere minutes since I was last buried inside her. It wasn't enough. I needed her again.

Needed her forever.

"You already have, Samuel." She covered her heart with her hand, her dark eyes overflowing with devotion. "In here."

Groaning, I lowered my lips to hers, our tongues briefly tangling. I slowly snaked down her body, leaving hot kisses on every inch of her, finally coming to a stop as I settled between her legs.

"You sure?" I asked as I uncapped the marker, bringing it up to the sensitive flesh by her hipbone.

"Yes." Her response came out breathy, her eyes unwavering as she watched me draw the symbol of my unconditional love on her.

"Are you okay?"

Imogene's voice cut through like a sharp knife. It took me few seconds to remember where I was.

When I was.

"Sorry," I said, a bit dazed. "Just went somewhere else for a minute." I handed her the tray now that she had a firm hold on her board.

"Thanks."

I forced a shallow nod and turned away, hastily collecting my newspaper and coffee before striding in the opposite direction, needing to put as much distance between us as possible.

That tattoo didn't change anything. It didn't *mean* anything.

She probably got it so she wouldn't feel guilty about moving on with her life.

Well, I didn't have that luxury.

It was time she finally felt my pain.

Time they all did.

CHAPTER FIVE

Imogene

"I'm sorry I can't stay and go to your first game," Liam said as he walked me to my car Saturday morning.

While I normally didn't like him spending the night, I felt uneasy after receiving that necklace. Whomever sent it knew the address of the townhouse I'd only been living in for a few weeks. As if that weren't unsettling enough, upon closer inspection of the box, I noticed there wasn't a shipping label.

Which could have only meant one thing.

This person didn't send it in the mail.

He left it at my front door.

He saw where I lived.

I would have felt better if it *had* been shipped. There was comfort in distance. Instead, this person had physically found my home. Stood on the front porch. Invaded my safe space.

Because of that, I didn't feel comfortable staying by myself, so I invited Liam to spend the night, blaming the wine he'd consumed.

I didn't tell him the *real* reason I wanted him to stay.

If I'd informed him someone left a box from my mother's bakery on my doorstep and it contained an exact replica of the heart necklace I once wore every day, he'd cancel all his meetings for the next week and insist on staying by my side.

Hell, he'd probably have me moved into his house before the end of the day.

That was the last thing I wanted.

"I've got a dinner in New York I can't miss," Liam explained.

"I'm fine," I assured him. "Especially now that I finally have an actual bed to sleep in. It would have taken me another few weeks to put that together."

"Why do I get the feeling those boxes will still be in the garage next weekend, too?" He pinched the bridge of his nose.

"Because you know me so well."

"That I do."

As we approached my car, he pulled me in for one more hug and touched a kiss to my cheek.

A sudden chill trickled down my spine, but it wasn't

from the feel of Liam's lips on my skin. Instead, the same sensation of being watched creeped over me.

Pushing out of Liam's embrace, I nervously scanned the street for anything that appeared out of place.

But like last night, there was nothing unusual.

That still didn't dampen the unease filling me.

"Are you sure you're okay?" Liam asked, sweeping his concerned gaze over me. "You seem...jumpy."

"I'm fine. I just drank a bit too much wine last night. I'll be better once I get more coffee in me." I lifted my travel mug to my lips, savoring the robust flavor.

"Are you sure?"

"Yes, I'm sure." I rolled my eyes, feigning annoyance, then reached for my car door.

Before I could touch the handle, Liam beat me to it, opening the door and helping me in. Once I was settled, he gently closed the door behind me. I cranked the engine and lowered the window.

"Thanks again for everything."

"Anytime, Gin."

I shifted the car into reverse and backed out onto the street, waving to Liam as I pulled away from my house.

Finally alone, I expelled a long breath, relishing in the first moment of solitude I'd had since surfing this morning.

The ocean was one of the few places I always managed to find peace and serenity. Bobbing up and down on my board when the world was still dark, waiting for the perfect wave to ride into shore. No phone. No laptop. Just me, my board, and the vast expanse of ocean.

After last night, I needed some time on the water more than anything.

I never expected to see *him* again.

To see those eyes again.

The shade of blue was so similar to Samuel's.

Even more so this morning, since I was able to get a much closer view than I did yesterday.

As I gazed into those haunting eyes, it felt as if I'd been transported back in time.

Especially when I saw him doing a crossword puzzle, just like we once did together.

But Samuel Tate was gone.

Over five years had passed since he disappeared without a trace, apart from the blood staining the driver's seat of his abandoned car. According to the police, he'd been shot by one of the kids in the teen program he'd founded.

But Jonah Pruitt didn't seem the type. He'd repeatedly claimed he was innocent, that he was being framed, even when a gun containing his fingerprints was found in a dumpster mere feet from Samuel's abandoned car.

The one thing they never found was Samuel's body, though. It was as if he had vanished into thin air, leaving behind only a pool of blood containing his DNA.

Maybe that was why I often questioned whether he was really dead. It didn't matter that every medical professional claimed the amount of blood he lost was too much for anyone to survive.

A part of me still hoped he was alive, despite the improbability.

Could my mystery man be Samuel? Or was running into someone with similar eyes merely a sign that it was time to let him go?

After all, this was why I'd moved to California. To finally move on with my life. To give myself the fresh start I needed.

The last thing I needed was to fall back into my old patterns, all because I saw a man who bore practically no resemblance to Samuel doing a crossword puzzle. Hell, even his voice was different — harsh and curt with not so much as a hint of the smooth tone that once lulled me to sleep.

"It wasn't him," I told myself, repeating the mantra as I navigated through the weekend traffic in downtown San Diego.

By the time I pulled into the stadium parking lot, I'd essentially expunged the idea from my mind, the bustling energy of game day replacing my unease.

I'd always loved soccer. In another life, I would have loved to play professionally.

Unfortunately, I'd been born with a heart defect that

required surgery when I was mere weeks old. While I was able to live a relatively normal life, thanks to early surgical prevention, I did have some limitations. And those limitations included not putting too much stress on my heart. At least not to the extent required to make it in the pros.

Instead, I pushed myself to do the next best thing. Be on the training team as a physical therapist. It was the perfect way for me to put my love of the game to use in a professional capacity without risking my health.

Approaching the therapy room in the bowels of the stadium, I held my ID card up to the pad, and the door buzzed, granting me entry. The lights flickered to life as I walked toward my desk, pulling my laptop out of my bag so I could review the notes I'd made during yesterday's practice.

"Knock, knock," a voice sang mere seconds after I settled in.

I looked away from the screen to see the office assistant, Abby, standing in the doorway, pushing a rolling cart.

"Got some mail for you."

When she grabbed a box with the familiar logo of my mother's bakery emblazoned on its side, my breath caught.

All I could do was stare at the ominous package as she approached, feeling like the room was closing in around me. She set the box on the corner of my desk, then left without another word.

My heart thrashed in my ears, my stomach churning. I didn't want to open it. Wanted to throw it away and pretend I never saw it.

But the last thing I needed on a game day was a distraction.

If I didn't open this box, I would most certainly be distracted.

I may be distracted anyway, but this way I'd know what this box contained.

Opening the top drawer of my desk, I pulled out a letter opener and sliced through the tape. With trembling hands, I removed the white bakery box from the package and set it in front of me, a glimmer of hope filling me when I felt its weight. It was much heavier than the package I'd received yesterday. Maybe it really *was* from my mother.

I cut through the twine and lifted the lid, exhaling in relief to find a note from my mama and stepdad wishing me luck, as well as a few dozen cookies.

Even better, they were my favorite flavor — peanut butter and jelly.

The sweet aroma wafted out of the box, making my stomach growl. I grabbed one and took a bite, moaning in pleasure.

"Sorry to bother you again," Abby said, peeking her

head into my office. "I missed this one. It was buried on the bottom."

I waved her in and she handed me an overnight envelope.

"Would you like a cookie?" I gestured toward the open box. "They're from my mom's bakery. You haven't lived until you've tried one of her peanut butter and jelly cookies."

"Those smell amazing." She grabbed one and took a bite. "And taste even better."

"They're my favorite."

"They might be mine, too." With a smile, she retreated from my office as I pulled the tab on the envelope, expecting to find the reports I'd requested from one of the players' outside physical therapists.

Instead, the only thing it contained was a necklace exactly like the one I'd received last night.

CHAPTER SIX

Imogene

"How did you hear about this place again?" I asked Melanie as she tugged me down a packed sidewalk in downtown San Diego.

Photographers lined the area with their cameras ready, hoping to catch a glimpse of one of the many celebrities I noticed heading inside what appeared to be a swanky club.

"Got an invitation earlier in the week. The benefit of working for an entertainment management firm. Don't you wish you went that route instead of physical therapy?" She waggled her brows before she scrunched up her nose. "Then again, you did just spend an entire year working on baseball players for your residency. What I wouldn't give to see some of those guys naked. I have my theories on which players are packing some serious heat in their jockstraps."

"I didn't see them naked," I reminded her with a laugh.

Although there were quite a few who tried to show off their goods when I was working on post-game therapy with them.

It was one of the reasons I wanted to work for a women's soccer team instead of accept a one-year contract with the baseball team in Atlanta. Not only did I want to know I got the job based on my qualifications, something I'd always wonder, since my step-father was Lachlan Hale, a former star pitcher for Atlanta. I also wanted a more...welcoming environment. Not that the staff in Atlanta wasn't welcoming. They were. But being a woman in a male-dominated career was definitely challenging.

"Whatever you say." Melanie rolled her eyes.

"Lachlan would have castrated them for even thinking of trying anything with me. You know how protective he can be."

"That I do."

Melanie and I met in college when I moved into an off-campus apartment across the hall. We'd formed an instant bond and, over the course of the next several years, became practically inseparable.

After she finished law school and accepted a job in

Beverly Hills, I missed having someone who understood me so well nearby, especially since it was mere months after Samuel's death. Now that I was here, I looked forward to making up for lost time, even if I almost bailed tonight after receiving a second necklace in so many days.

But the last thing I wanted was to go home and over-think what this could mean. Instead, I came out, intending to drink enough that I'd forget all about the necklaces.

As we approached the entrance, the pulsing beat of the music grew louder. A pair of imposing men in dark suits stood guard, but they didn't seem to intimidate Melanie, who exuded confidence as she gave them her name. Based on the A-list celebrities I'd seen walk into this place, I half expected them to turn us away. Then again, many of those A-list celebrities were Melanie's clients.

One of the guards stepped aside, permitting us entry, and Melanie looped her arm through mine, leading me passed a dimly lit area filled with oversized leather couches and toward a sleek, modern bar where attractive men and women expertly flipped bottles, mixing drinks with precision.

After giving the bartender our order, I scanned the large space. I recognized nearly every person here. Actors. Athletes. Models. Even a few politicians.

I was actually surprised Liam wasn't here. He usually loved attending this kind of thing. As much as I adored him and was proud of everything he'd accomplished, he had a tendency to be fixated on being part of the "in" crowd.

As a child, he had a difficult home life. His mother was only sixteen when she got pregnant with him, and her overly strict parents had no problem reminding him he was a bastard every chance they got.

It only got worse when my father killed his mother, leaving him to be raised by two people who despised him.

I still couldn't help but feel guilty about everything he had to endure, all because my sperm donor took away the one person who cared about him. But as Liam had repeatedly assured me, it wasn't my fault. If anything, all the shit he went through forced him to work even harder to be successful, if for no other reason than to prove his grandparents wrong.

To shove his success in their faces.

And that was exactly what he did.

The bartender handed us our drinks, and we thanked him, leaving a generous tip. Then we made our way toward a vacant high-top table overlooking the dance floor that was packed with people moving to a hypnotic beat. I would have given anything to find somewhere to sit, considering my feet were already killing me.

"To finally being together again." Melanie raised her manhattan toward me.

"To being together again," I repeated with a smile, clinking my glass with hers before taking a sip of my old fashioned. As I did, a shiver ran down my spine, that same sensation of being watched creeping over me.

I discreetly surveyed my surroundings, my eyes locking on a man dressed in all black standing on the opposite side of the dance floor. His gaze bore into me, something sinister about him. After a tense moment, he looked away and continued to scan the club. That was when I noticed the earpiece tucked into his ear.

Of course.

He was one of the security guards.

He wasn't just watching *me*.

He was watching everyone.

"So tell me," Melanie began, leaning toward me so I could hear. She smoothed a few waves of her dark hair behind her ear. "How was your first week at your job? How's your townhouse coming along? Or are you still living out of boxes and sleeping on a mattress?"

"The boxes are still packed, but I'm no longer sleeping on a mattress, thanks to Liam."

"Let me guess. He sent a bunch of big, strong handymen to your place to assemble all that furniture we bought last weekend. I hope to god at least one of them was easy on the eyes."

"He didn't send any handymen."

Her brow furrowed. "Then—"

"*He* showed up last night and helped me put a bunch of it together."

Melanie choked on her drink, some of the liquid spraying out of her nose. She grabbed a cocktail napkin and dabbed at her face. Regardless, her makeup was still impeccable, as if a professional had applied it.

"You're shitting me."

"I certainly wasn't expecting to see him, either." I rolled my eyes.

"Oh, I'm not surprised he showed up. He adores you and would do anything for you. I simply can't imagine Liam Pierce putting together furniture. It seems so... beneath him."

"He used to help us assemble furniture all the time."

"That was before he had more money than sense." She took another sip of her drink. "Speaking of more money than sense."

Scowling, she set her glass onto the table and nodded toward a group of people sitting on a pair of couches a few feet away.

Actually, that wasn't entirely accurate. It was more like a harem, a handful of models hanging all over an actor I recognized.

"Be grateful Liam hasn't turned into someone like Atlas Wolfe," she remarked with a hint of bitterness.

"Some days I feel more like an overpaid babysitter than an intelligent woman with a law degree." With a long sigh, she downed nearly all of her drink in a few gulps. "Time to go remind him that he's one bad story away from being fired off his current series."

"'May the odds be ever in your favor,'" I quoted from one of our favorite books as I tilted my glass toward her.

She paused, raising her arm to the sky with three fingers extended, much like Katniss Everdeen did.

Then she spun on her heels, a woman on a mission.

I didn't know how she did it. I'd hate having to cater to the whims of high-strung celebrities. It was bad enough having to deal with some of the baseball players' egos during my residency. That was nothing compared to what Melanie had to put up with, though.

As much as she may have complained, I knew she loved it.

I continued to sip on my drink, trying not to feel out of place amongst all the actors, models, and politicians, when a body rammed into me, causing the liquor to spill down the front of my dress.

At least I'd worn black.

"Oh, shit," a man in his twenties slurred, reeking of booze and too much cologne. "I'm *so* sorry." He grabbed a napkin off the table and dabbed at my chest.

I quickly stepped back, pushing down my irritation

not just with him, but also with his friends who were openly gawking at my breasts.

"I can handle it." I snatched my clutch and searched the room for Melanie. She was no longer in the lounge area where her client was seconds ago.

Neither was her client.

I squinted, attempting to find her in the darkened space, finally spotting her in a corner, seemingly in the middle of an intense conversation with Atlas Wolfe.

When she noticed me, I mouthed *bathroom*. She nodded, holding up two fingers. Then I weaved through the throngs of people until I reached the narrow hallway that led to the restrooms.

The good thing about Melanie dragging me to an upscale club was the amenities. Instead of flimsy paper towels or a broken hand dryer, there were soft cloth towels and powerful blow dryers at my disposal. If someone were to spill their drink on me, this was the best place for it to happen.

Once my dress was relatively dry, I sat in front of the vanity, if for no other reason than to give my feet a rest. Opening my clutch, I took a moment to freshen my makeup, reapplying my eyeliner and lip gloss. Then I stood and slipped back into the hallway, the music growing louder with every step.

"Excuse me, miss," a voice called out from behind me.

Startled, I turned around to see a man of around my age holding up a tube of the same brand of lip gloss I used.

"I think you dropped this." He narrowed his dark gaze on me, not taking his eyes off me for a second.

There was something unnerving about it, but I quickly brushed it off. I needed to stop thinking everyone was watching me.

Approaching him, I grabbed the tube from him. "Thanks."

Then I continued back down the hallway once more.

But when I opened my clutch and saw my lip gloss was already in there, I came to an abrupt stop.

A sinking sensation formed in the pit of my stomach as I stared at this other tube, a voice in my head telling me not to open it.

But I needed to.

Even though I couldn't shake the feeling I already knew what was inside.

With trembling hands, I uncapped the container and tipped it upside down. Another necklace identical to the previous ones I'd received fell onto my palm. It probably only weighed a few ounces, but it felt like it was crushing me.

Whirling around, I focused on the retreating figure as he pushed open the rear emergency door and disappeared outside. Every rational instinct I possessed cautioned against following him.

I needed answers, though. Needed to know who the fuck was sending me these damn necklaces.

Cursing my choice of shoes, I hurried down the hallway as fast as I could, bursting through the door and emerging into a dark alley, the stench of urine and garbage assaulting my senses.

I frantically scanned the area for the man who'd given me this necklace when an unexpected force slammed into me.

The jarring impact of my head hitting the hard brick wall left me momentarily disoriented, my brain struggling to clear itself of the confusion and pain.

But when a body pressed against mine, fight or flight kicked in.

Summoning my strength, I tried to recall everything Samuel taught me. He always said that most men chose women because they viewed us as easy targets. That the best way to fight back was to use the element of surprise to my advantage. Make him think I didn't pose a threat.

"Don't hurt me. I'll give you whatever you want."

"Is that right?"

My muscles trembled when I felt his warm breath on my neck. A hard object pressed against my lower back, causing bile to rise in my throat.

"Please," I whimpered, fear and desperation flooding through me.

"I do love it when a girl begs." He pushed a knee between my legs to spread them apart. "This wasn't part of the plan, but may as well get some extra payment for my troubles."

I blinked repeatedly, trying to figure out what he meant by that. What plan? And extra payment? Was he paid to come after me? I couldn't waste time dwelling on that, though. I needed to act.

I discreetly put some space between myself and the wall, giving me some wiggle room to maneuver. Thankfully, it was enough to allow me to do what I needed, and I quickly spun around, landing a quick jab to his nose and a knee to his groin.

"You fucking bitch," he groaned, releasing me as he clutched himself, blood spilling down his face. "Easy mark, my ass."

Without hesitation, I ran as fast as my heels would allow. But in my panic, my ankle gave out, and I fell onto the ground. The thunder of footsteps behind me spurred me to get up, but before I could, he was on top of me. Grabbing a fistful of hair, he yanked my head back, pressing a knife against my throat.

"Scream and I'll cut you. Got it?"

The sharp sting of the blade forced me to hold my

breath, my muscles locked in fear. I swallowed hard, trying not to make any sudden movements.

With a trembling voice, I managed to whisper, "Yes."

"Good." He brought his lips closer to my ear. "Now, are you going to play nice?"

I squeezed my eyes shut, not wanting to give up so easily. But when he pressed the knife even harder against my skin and drew blood, I didn't have a choice.

Biting back tears, I parted my lips, my body recoiling at the thought of surrendering to this monster. My compliance was on the tip of my tongue when a commotion erupted nearby, pulling his attention away from me.

In one swift motion, the weight that had been crushing me was gone, the unmistakable sound of cracking bones echoing in the alley.

I scrambled to my feet, finding an imposing figure standing over my attacker, who now lay in a heap on the ground. I didn't know if he was dead or just unconscious.

Before I could worry about that, the figure turned toward me and his piercing blue eyes met mine.

"You," I exhaled, my breaths coming quicker as the world spun around me, my heartbeat erratic.

Concern widened his gaze. He erased the distance between us, sweeping me into his arms and pressing a hand against my heart.

Just like Samuel once did.

That was the last thing I thought before the dizziness consumed me and everything went black.

CHAPTER SEVEN

Imogene

"Good news, Ms. Prescott," a man wearing blue scrubs and a white coat announced, walking into the hospital room where I'd been subjected to various tests over the past hour.

By the time I finally came around after fainting, I was already being lifted out of the back seat of the mystery man's SUV and carried into the emergency room. Regardless of what I attempted to tell him or any of the medical staff, that the dizziness and fainting spell was simply because of a sudden increase in adrenaline from the attack, they refused to listen.

"The results from all your tests came back clear with no abnormalities."

I bit my lip, fighting the urge to tell him I predicted

as much. This wasn't my first rodeo. I would have known if there was a problem with my heart. I was fine, all things considered.

"You do have a mild concussion, though. Nothing to be too concerned with, but I want to keep you here for observation until morning. I recommend you follow up with your cardiologist within the next week."

"Of course."

By this point, I was all too familiar with the drill. Whenever I was involved in anything remotely stressful, even something as minor as a fender bender, I was forced to endure a myriad of tests with my cardiologist to make sure there weren't any adverse complications to my heart.

There never were, but because I had several open heart surgeries before I was even ten years old, I would always be at a higher risk of having heart-related complications.

"I'll let you get some rest. A nurse will be in to check on you shortly. I can also send your friend back in, if you'd like."

"Yes. Thank you."

He gave me one last nod and stepped into the hallway, closing the door behind him. Once I was finally alone, I fell back against the uncomfortable pillows and sighed.

What a way to end my first week of work. Spending

the night in the hospital definitely wasn't on my bingo card for the day. I was beginning to wonder if maybe I should have just moved in with Liam.

Would that have changed anything, though? The necklaces hadn't only been sent to my house. I'd also received one at work, as well as at the club. Whoever this guy was, he was able to get to me anywhere. Anytime.

No doubt he would have been able to get to me at Liam's house, too.

A loud, determined knock ripped through the relative silence, jolting me out of my thoughts.

"Come in," I called without looking up, assuming it was Melanie.

But when the door opened, it wasn't my best friend who entered.

It was my mystery man.

His tall, broad-shouldered figure filled the doorway, his black suit perfectly tailored to his frame. His dark hair was styled messily, his intense gaze lingering on me before flickering around the room.

"I'm sorry for barging in, but I..." He shook his head, his expression strained. He paused for a beat, taking a moment to collect himself, then focused his eyes on mine. "I wanted to make sure you were okay."

"I'm fine," I assured him. "Doctors tend to overreact because I had a heart valve replaced when I was younger. But I'm okay."

He closed his eyes, his shoulders falling slightly.

It was a curious reaction for a man who was essentially a stranger.

"I brought you a change of clothes." He held up a crisp, white shopping bag. "I figured the last thing you'd want to do after spending the night in a hospital is go home in the dress you were wearing. Don't get me wrong," he rambled nervously, which I found oddly comforting.

It made him appear less intimidating. More human.

"You looked great in that dress. Stunning really." He raked his gaze over me, his pupils flaming as if I were the sexiest woman he'd ever seen.

Not as if I were wearing a hospital gown, my blonde hair a disheveled mess on the top of my head.

"You just seem like more of a yoga pants and t-shirt kind of girl. There's also a phone charger in there, since I noticed your cell was dead."

"Thank you..." I trailed off, my brow creasing in confusion. "I'm sorry. I don't even know your name."

A chuckle filled the room, low and raspy. "Gideon. Gideon Saint."

"Ginny Prescott." I extended my hand toward him.

When he took it in his, his thumb gently caressing my knuckles, a jolt of electricity shot through me, my pulse kicking up. It was a simple touch, but something about the way his hand fit with mine was so damn familiar.

Like I'd been here before.

I stared into his brilliant blue eyes that seemed out of place. They didn't belong on a face with a square jaw, chiseled cheekbones, crooked nose, and a three-day scruff. They belonged to a man with unkempt brown hair whose presence once lit up my entire world.

Even so, I couldn't ignore the way my body buzzed to life from his touch.

Like it remembered something about his skin against mine.

Or maybe it was due to the fact that he was an incredibly attractive man with a sinful smile and I hadn't had sex, apart from with my vibrator, in nearly a year.

"I prefer Imogene..." He glanced at the hospital bracelet on my wrist, my full first name prominent. "If you don't mind my saying."

I once did, too. My mama named me after my great grandmother, who she had a special bond with. When I was growing up, she would regale me with such vivid stories about spending her summers at their old farmhouse on a lake. It was where my mama developed her love of baking. She'd told me of her tenacious spirit, quick wit, and kind heart.

I liked to think I possessed those same characteristics.

But after my sperm donor made headlines for his

horrific crimes, then escaped prison and abducted me, my name had been plastered on every media outlet across the country. Having a unique name like Imogene didn't help matters.

After that, I started going by Ginny, not wanting the friends I hoped to make in college to realize who I was.

Being a teen girl was difficult enough.

It wasn't until I met Samuel that I allowed anyone to call me Imogene again. I didn't even let Liam call me that.

But Samuel had always been different. He encouraged me to take back my life. Not allow my sperm donor to continue to control me.

Not allow the guilt I still saddled myself with to control me, either.

"Thank you."

"Of course." He dropped his hold on me and stepped back, his expression turning even and detached, a complete shift. "I just wanted to let you know that a detective will be stopping by in the morning. He'd wanted to speak with you tonight, but I sent him away. You've already been through enough."

"Shouldn't I give them a description now so they can catch the guy?"

"You can rest assured he won't be able to hurt you or anyone else ever again." He pinned me with a stare, something dark and dangerous flashing in his eyes.

I didn't bother asking him to clarify what he meant. I knew. After all, I'd heard the unmistakable sound of a neck being snapped. Saw his lifeless body in a heap on the ground.

Instead of feeling horrified over the idea that this man was able to take a life with the efficiency of a trained killer, it didn't scare me.

If anything, it made me more curious about who Gideon Saint was.

I made a mental note to ask Melanie. If he had as much money as I sensed he did based on the designer suit and Tag Heuer watch on his wrist, she'd probably know something about him.

"Well, thank you. For everything. If you didn't find me when you did, I—"

"Don't."

His gruff tone caused me to snap my mouth shut.

"Don't what?"

"Look at me like that."

"Like what?"

"Like I'm a hero. I'm not. Far from it. The sooner you realize that, the better off you'll be."

"If you're not a hero, why did you save me?"

"Because I want something."

Alarm bells rang in my head, but that wasn't enough for me to back down, even though all reason told me the best thing I could do was keep my distance.

"And what's that?" I asked with a trembling voice.

His mouth curved into a sinister smile.

But before he could respond, the sound of determined footsteps cut through. I snapped my head toward the doorway just as Liam barreled inside, wrapping me in his arms.

"I came as soon as Mel called." His voice was hoarse with worry as he squeezed me tightly, his panic palpable. "Who the hell did this?" He pulled back, but didn't release me, his grip on my biceps firm. "I want names. Want to make sure this guy rots in prison for the rest of his pathetic life."

"That won't be necessary," Gideon stated in a commanding voice before I had a chance to respond. He stepped toward Liam, his expression hardened and borderline severe. "The problem's already taken care of."

"Who are you?" Liam squared his shoulders, narrowing his gaze on Gideon.

Melanie appeared in the doorway, slipping inside and offering me an apologetic look. She didn't have to say a single word for me to know what she was telling me, that she tried to stop Liam from interrupting.

"Gideon Saint."

Liam's gaze widened, and he did a double take. It was obvious he'd heard of him.

"Gideon Saint, as in the CEO of Growth Ventures?" Liam asked.

"The one and the same," Gideon responded, his demeanor still distant.

"I've heard a lot about you." He extended his hand. "Liam Pierce."

"I'm aware." He placed his hand in Liam's, his jaw clenched.

My eyes darted between the two men, something flickering in Gideon's stare, as if he struggled to contain his irritation. Or anger. But it was more than that. More than disgust. Almost like hatred.

"Gideon helped me tonight," I explained, hoping to break through the growing tension in the room.

I half expected Gideon to break every finger in Liam's hand. Based on what I'd witnessed him do tonight, he was more than capable of doing just that.

And worse.

Luckily, he didn't, releasing his hold on Liam.

"When the guy attacked me, I tried to fight him."

"What were you doing in some alley?" Liam shifted his attention back to me. "What the hell were you thinking?" He paced the length of the room, tugging on his sandy hair. "If something had happened to you..." He stopped in his tracks, approaching me and taking my hand back in his. "Haven't we already lost enough? I can't stomach the idea of losing you, too."

I felt the heat of Gideon's stare from across the room, his irritation simmering just beneath the surface. Why did he seem so irked by Liam? Did they have dealings with each other professionally? Liam was on the board of one of the largest media conglomerates in existence. It sounded like Gideon was well-known in the business world himself. Was there more to the tension than that?

"What are you doing here anyway?" I tilted my head. "Aren't you supposed to be in New York?"

He looked away. "Some last-minute business came up that required me to be in Los Angeles. I was about to take off for New York when I got Mel's phone call. I headed straight here."

"You didn't need to do that. As you can see, I'm fine."

"You're in the damn hospital, Gin. I wouldn't call that fine."

"You know how these things go. They have to err on the side of caution and subject me to dozens of unnecessary tests."

"You should err on the side of caution, too. And that includes not disappearing out of the back of a club into a goddamn alley!"

"I know. I don't need you to treat me like I'm a child. I just..." I expelled a breath, glancing at the clock on the wall to see it was nearing two in the morning..

The last thing I wanted was to get into everything I'd kept from both Melanie and Liam. I'd been up for almost twenty-four hours and was bone tired.

"I'm sure Ms. Prescott would like to get some rest,"

Gideon stated with authority, as if able to read my thoughts. Then his expression softened as his eyes met mine. "I'm glad you're okay."

"Thank you."

He held my gaze for a protracted beat, then he turned toward Liam. "Mr. Pierce." He gave him a curt nod before smiling at Melanie. "Ms. Burnham."

"Mr. Saint," she responded.

An awkward silence filled the room as we all watched Gideon retreat into the hallway.

"Why don't you come to Ginny's birthday party?" Liam called out just as he was about to disappear from view.

I darted my eyes toward Liam, his invitation catching me off guard. Why was he inviting Gideon to my birthday party?

Then again, Liam wasn't really throwing it in my honor. It was more for him to put on a show for all his wealthy friends, further confirmation that Gideon Saint was someone worth knowing, at least in Liam's mind.

"We'd love to have you."

When Liam placed his hand on my shoulder and squeezed, I gave him a questioning look. Why was he trying to imply we were an item? Did he feel threatened by Gideon?

"It's okay if you can't," I told him. "I'm sure you have a busy schedule."

"I do, but I'm more than happy to make time for you, Imogene."

The way my name rolled off his tongue sent a shiver down my spine. Soft. Sensual. Seductive.

"She prefers to go by Ginny," Liam said.

"And I prefer to let the lady speak for herself," Gideon snipped back before reaching into the inside pocket of his suit and handing Liam a card. "Send me the details. I look forward to getting to know you better." He looked at me. "Imogene."

He allowed my name to hang in the air for a few more seconds. Then he disappeared down the hallway.

But even after he was gone, his presence lingered in the room like a phantom, leaving me confused, captivated, and intrigued about who Gideon Saint really was.

And why I felt I knew him.

CHAPTER EIGHT

Gideon

"Who is he?" I barked out the second I stepped into the office of my oceanfront villa mere blocks away from Imogene's townhouse.

I was lucky to find somewhere so close on such quick notice. That was another lesson I'd learned over the past year.

When you had money, people bent over backwards to give you what you wanted.

And I wanted this house, if for no other reason than because Liam had hoped to buy it for himself. Too bad the owner accepted a different offer — mine.

"Hello to you, too," Henry snipped back, his tone dripping with sarcasm.

The glare I gave him let him know I wasn't in a joking mood. Not after Imogene was attacked.

I'd been watching her since she walked into that club. I knew she'd be there. After all, I was the one who made sure Melanie received an invitation, the perks of holding a ten-percent stake in the company that owned the club.

But when I noticed Imogene follow someone out the back door, a sinking feeling formed in the pit of my stomach. Despite not wanting her to be aware of my presence, I knew I'd regret it if I didn't follow her.

When I saw her on the ground with that asshole holding a knife to her throat, I saw red, the instincts I'd picked up after years of fighting for my life on a daily basis kicking in.

"What do you know?" I demanded, my patience already wearing thin from the night I'd had.

When I realized the guy whose neck I snapped hadn't been the same one I observed approach Imogene in the club, I had Henry work his magic to get me a name, which he easily did, and then some.

"Name's Benjamin Astor." He handed me a folder.

I snatched it from him and headed toward the leather sofa, lowering myself onto it as I sifted through the extensive background report.

One thing was certain. I was damn glad I took a risk

on Henry's idea for a cyber security startup several years ago and invested in it. In the years that I was supposedly dead, his company went from making six figures a year to over ten. And because I'd given him the capital he needed to get his company off the ground, he'd made me an equal partner, with an equal share of the profits.

After I finally escaped the hell I'd been living in, only to learn the woman I fought to stay alive for was sleeping with the enemy, the first thing I did was pay a visit to the one person I felt I could trust.

The one person I knew would want revenge, too.

Henry Fontaine.

He was one of the many foster brothers I'd had throughout my years of being shuffled from home to home. Despite the instability of our childhoods, we never lost touch.

In fact, when I'd found success with my gaming platform and started my charity to help at-risk teens, he didn't hesitate in agreeing to volunteer.

He'd once been one of those at-risk teens himself before he enlisted in the military at eighteen.

Like me, he'd formed a close bond with Jonah. Probably even more so. Much like Henry, he'd shown a keen interest in cyber security, even if his initial interest was more to learn how to hack into various computer systems.

Because Henry knew Jonah so well, he struggled to believe he would have killed me.

When I showed up on his doorstep and told him what *really* happened, Henry didn't hesitate. If anything, he was eager to make them all pay, too.

To finally clear Jonah's name.

Truthfully, none of this would have been possible without Henry's ability to find any information I needed. While I'd studied engineering and computer science, thanks to a wrestling scholarship I'd been awarded, my knowledge of computer systems paled in comparison to Henry. It was why the NSA had hoped to recruit him after he left the military.

He almost worked for them.

Until I gave him the funding he needed to start his own firm.

"He's another foster system success story." Henry gave me a sarcastic look, his feelings about the foster system in this country matching my own.

Some kids were lucky and were placed in great homes. And there were a lot of great homes.

Unfortunately, we hadn't been so lucky. It got to the point that I stopped unpacking what meager possessions I owned, knowing it was only a matter of time until I became too much for my new family.

Thankfully, Henry and I found each other.

"Enlisted in the army after high school, but was given a psychological discharge after a year. After that, he worked a bunch of menial jobs. Janitor. Fast food. Mail room. Golf course maintenance. As you can see, he hasn't held the same job for more than a few months."

I nodded, processing the bullet points of what was contained within these pages.

"What's his connection to Imogene?"

"On paper, there isn't one. There's no evidence he's ever visited Atlanta or California, until recently. His last known address is in New Mexico. There were charges on his credit card in Albuquerque just a few days ago, so he hasn't been in town long."

"But...," I prodded, sensing he'd found something.

"I had one of my guys go to his apartment before the local police got there." He turned his laptop toward me.

I stood, a heat washing over my face as my eyes fell on a shrine to Imogene's father, the wall plastered with newspaper clippings regaling his heinous crimes. But the most prominent headline was Imogene's abduction when she was fourteen, as well as a closeup photo of the necklace she once wore.

The necklace she'd been sent three times over the past several days.

"Any ties to the guy who attacked her in the alley? Glen Roy?" I asked, not wanting my emotions to get the better of me. Not now. Not when I was on the brink of putting a bullet in this guy's head.

"I couldn't find anything connecting them. It could have just been a coincidence that she chased Astor into an alley, and Roy happened to be there and attacked her, causing Astor to flee."

"You know how I feel about coincidences."

Henry nodded. "That there's no such thing."

"Exactly."

My mind whirled as I stared into the distance, processing everything Henry just shared. Hell, processing everything that happened tonight. From watching Imogene follow some guy out of the club, to running out to the alley, to killing the asshole who'd attacked her, to unexpectedly seeing Liam at the hospital.

That was what unsettled me the most. He was the last person I expected to see there. I wasn't the only one, either. According to Imogene, he was supposed to be in New York.

"Liam," I ground out.

"What does he have to do with this?"

"He was at the hospital."

"He was?" Henry's gaze widened as he ran a hand through his dark hair.

I nodded gravely.

"Shit. How did that go?"

"I managed not to kill him. At least not yet. But Imogene mentioned he was supposed to be in New York."

"And because he was at the hospital when he should have been on the opposite side of the country..." Henry began, narrowing his green eyes on me.

"It's suspicious. Or perhaps a bit too convenient for my liking. He claimed he had some last-minute business come up in Los Angeles, but I don't know..."

"You think the reason he wasn't in New York might be chained up down the hall right now?"

I could hear the skepticism in his voice. It was why I was glad to have him on my side. Henry was rational, clear-headed. He didn't let his emotions or feelings cloud his judgment.

He was often the voice of reason I needed.

I had a feeling I'd need him more in the days to come, as well.

"It's a possibility."

"But there are a dozen other possibilities, too. You said yourself that Imogene was often targeted by true crime fanatics who were obsessed with her father. Or religious zealots who insisted the child must pay for the sins of the father, or something like that. Based on what my guy uncovered at his apartment..."

"I understand that. But I don't know..." I shook my head. "I have a bad feeling about this. Just like I did all those years ago. I didn't listen to my gut back then, and it nearly cost me my life. I can't take that risk now. Not with Imogene's life. Which is why I want you to put some guys on her. Don't make it obvious, but make sure she's safe."

"Oh, really?" He leaned back into his chair and crossed his arms over his t-shirt. "I thought you didn't care about her."

"Just make sure nothing happens to her," I barked as I tossed the file back onto his desk.

Getting into my conflicted feelings about Imogene, especially after seeing that asshole put his hands on her tonight, was the last thing I wanted to do right now.

"If anyone so much looks at her the wrong way, I want to know about it."

He mock saluted me. "Whatever you say, boss."

With determined steps, I continued out of the office and down the long hallway, stopping in front of a secured door at the end.

After punching in my code, I pressed my thumb against the pad and the door buzzed. The instant I entered the dimly lit space, a chill settled over me, the stench of piss and vomit suffocating.

It brought back disturbing recollections of my own imprisonment, being kept in worse conditions than this, only let out to train or fight in death matches for the entertainment of sick fucks on the dark web. The mere thought of all the lives I had to take just to live to see another day made bile rise in my throat, but I quickly pushed down the memories. I refused to let this asshole see a single ounce of weakness.

"Wakey, wakey, Benji," I sang, approaching the slumped-over figure, his wrists bound together and attached to a thick chain secured to the reinforced wall.

I wasn't sure what my plan was in having Henry bring him here. I just knew he played a part in what happened to Imogene tonight.

And for that, he'd have to pay.

"Time to have a little chat."

When Benjamin didn't stir, I kicked his stomach, relishing in the sound of his pained grunt. He flung his eyes open, seemingly disoriented until he focused on me.

Raw panic replaced all traces of confusion.

"Morning, sunshine. Have a nice nap?"

"Where am I?" He tugged on his restraints, but it was useless.

"That's not important right now. All that *is* important is how much longer you'll be here. Which all depends on you."

"Me?"

I paced the length of the room, my leather shoes echoing against the concrete floor. Stopping in front of a workbench, I unfolded a leather knife roll. I made an elaborate show out of removing a knife and examining it before returning it to its protective sheath, continuing the process with several more.

And with each one, Benjamin's nerves increased, a wet stain soon appearing on his pants.

"Precisely," I said as I settled on a knife and returned to him. "You're going to tell me what you wanted with Imogene Prescott." I toyed with the blade, pressing it against my pointer finger to see how easily it drew blood.

It was certainly sharp.

I leaned toward him, dragging the knife up the inside of his leg, every muscle in his body tensing as I neared his groin. He tried to get away, but he couldn't, the shackles on his ankles preventing him from doing so.

"And you're going to tell me now."

"Please," he whimpered. "You need to understand."

"No, Benji." I tightened my grip on the knife and brought it up to his throat. Little droplets of blood escaped from where it dug into his skin. "The only thing I need to understand is that you were involved in an attack outside a club a few hours ago. And that woman you targeted? Let's just say I have a particular interest in assuring her safety for the time being."

"But I didn't touch her. I wasn't the one who attacked her."

"Maybe not, but you were involved. Your actions prompted her to follow you into the alley, at which point she was assaulted. Correct me if I'm wrong, but that *was* your intention. Was it not?"

"No. I swear to you. He promised me if I did what he asked, I could—"

"*Who* promised you?" I demanded, pressing the blade even harder against his throat.

His wide, panicked eyes locked on mine as his chin quivered. "I don't know his name. He approached me last week. Knew everything about me, man. Including..."

"Including about your shrine to a serial killer?"

"It's not him I care about."

"It's her," I finished, my nostrils flaring.

I fought against the urge to slice his throat right then and there, all reason momentarily leaving me at the mere thought of someone touching Imogene.

"He told me if I did something for him, he'd reward me."

"What did he ask you to do?"

"Deliver three necklaces."

"And your reward? What was it?"

His lips curved into a sickening grin as he replied, "Why, Imogene Prescott, of course. As long as I got her to follow me out of the club, she'd be mine. We were to take her to a cabin in the mountains and keep her out of sight."

"Glen Roy," I seethed, struggling to keep an even

head as the image of that bastard on top of Imogene flashed before my eyes. "You were working with him?"

"I suppose. I never met him until a few days ago."

"This guy who hired you... What did he look like?"

"Mid- to late-thirties. Dirty blonde hair. Wore expensive suits."

I straightened, setting the knife onto the workbench as I pulled my phone out of my pocket. With a few quick taps, I brought up a photo of Liam and held it in front of Benjamin.

"Is this him?" My voice dripped with barely contained anger.

"Yes."

"You're certain?"

"Yes." He quickly nodded. "That's him."

I clenched my fists, every muscle in my body vibrating with fury. Why would Liam hire this guy to send Imogene necklaces? And why would he plan for her to be attacked outside the club? What was his goal in wanting her kidnapped?

Regardless of his motive, I couldn't ignore that this situation presented me with an unexpected opportunity. One I'd be a fool not to use to my advantage.

After all, Liam had pinned my murder on an innocent man. He should know exactly how that felt.

"You know what, Benji..." I began with a smirk. "I do believe this could be the start of a beautiful friendship."

"F-friendship?" Benjamin repeated, blinking repeatedly. "Does that mean you're going to let me go?" He looked at me hopefully.

I barked out a laugh. "Not on your life. Unfortunately for you, I can't have anyone learning who I really am. Can't have you running to Liam Pierce about any of this."

"I swear. I won't tell him. If you let me go, you'll never see me again."

"That's a risk I simply can't afford. I do hope you can understand that."

He squeezed his eyes shut and a few tears fell down his cheeks. "So you're still going to kill me?"

"You've left me with no choice. But cheer up, Benji. Your death won't be in vain."

I stepped in front of the workbench and opened a drawer, putting on a pair of black rubber gloves. Then I went to the closet, examining the contents.

"Now what type of gun would Liam use to kill someone?" I mused, my eyes scanning the shelves filled with various weapons. "Glock 9 millimeter? Smith and Wesson 357? Colt 45? Ah, here it is. Pearl handle 38."

I grabbed the gun and checked the cylinder, making sure it was loaded before snapping it back in place.

"Liam was always a bit...extra. No doubt he'd want a gun that was the same."

I faced Benjamin, advancing toward him with my weapon aimed at his torso.

"No. Please. I'm sorry," he cried, his sobs overtaking him. "I didn't mean for this to happen. Didn't mean for her to get hurt."

"You should have thought about that beforehand."

I added pressure to the trigger and a deafening bang reverberated in the room as Benjamin's body went limp, blood pooling around him.

CHAPTER NINE

Imogene

"I can walk, ya know," I snipped out at Liam as he led me up to the front door of the massive house he bought in Rancho Santa Fe, his protective arm wrapped around my waist.

A gentle breeze rustled through the trees, kicking up the smell of freshly cut grass and fragrant flowers. Despite its opulence, this was the last place I wanted to be right now.

I wanted my home, regardless of its current state of disarray. Unfortunately, the doctor would only release me if I had someone agree to watch over me for the next twenty-four hours, so I was stuck going home with Liam.

"I know, Gin. I just..."

Coming to a stop by the front door, he exhaled a long

sigh and faced me, clutching my cheeks. He squeezed his eyes shut, resting his forehead against mine.

"You have no idea how scared I was when Melanie called. It didn't matter what assurances she gave me." When he met my gaze, concern and fear swirled in his dark orbs. "It brought back too many memories. Losing Samuel the way we did was bad enough. To learn you were attacked in an alley? It reminded me of the phone call I got when they found his car." He shook his head, trying to clear away the painful memories.

"You may think I'm overreacting. And maybe I am. But when it comes to you, there's no such thing. I can't bear the thought of getting another phone call like that. I can't lose you, too."

"And you won't," I assured him, pressing a hand to his cheek. "The guy who attacked me can't hurt me anymore."

"What about whoever gave you that damn necklace?" Liam shot back with a sharp edge to his voice, digging his fingers through his hair and messing it up.

The perfectly maintained appearance he usually kept was in disarray, his face unshaven and sandy hair askew. His designer suit now hung wrinkled on his form.

"They still haven't found him. He could be anywhere." He punched his code into the keypad in frustration.

Once the door buzzed, he stepped back, allowing me

to walk into his palatial estate. It seemed excessive for a home that wasn't his primary residence. I'd learned there was no such thing when it came to Liam Pierce. He had money and wanted everyone to know it.

He wanted his *grandparents* to know it.

"I still can't believe you didn't tell me about the necklaces," he murmured.

"I honestly thought it was just some fanatic," I lied.

The only upside to this guy approaching me in the club was all the security cameras inside. By the time the detective came to take my statement this morning, he already had a name — Benjamin Astor.

When the police searched his apartment in Albuquerque, they found evidence he'd been fascinated by my father's story, and me, in particular.

But what continued to baffle investigators was their inability to find any connection between Astor and the man who'd attacked me, Glen Roy.

So far, they appeared to be two isolated, unconnected events.

Although my gut said otherwise.

"I've been telling you for years, Gin. You need to be more careful," Liam admonished as we walked into the formal living area.

A crystal chandelier hung from the high ceiling, casting a warm glow over the room. The large windows overlooked a stunning swimming pool, a pristine lawn just beyond it, all of it with a magnificent view of the ocean in the distance.

"I'm *fine*, Liam."

"This time. But what happens the next time someone tries something like this?"

With an exaggerated roll of my eyes, I pushed away from him and made my way toward the kitchen. "You're overreacting."

A woman in a maid's uniform approached, handing me a steaming mug. "Coffee, Ms. Prescott?"

I had no doubt Liam had already told her how I preferred my coffee.

"Thank you." I took the mug from her, albeit reluctantly. I didn't need someone waiting on me, making my coffee. I could do that myself.

"I think you should move in here," Liam announced once we were alone.

I gave him a warning glare from over my coffee mug.

"I'm *not* moving in with you, Liam. The only reason I agreed to stay here today is because the doc wouldn't discharge me unless someone agreed to keep an eye on me until tomorrow morning. Unfortunately, Melanie had to get back to LA for an event tonight. Otherwise, I would have just had her stay with me."

"Stop being so damn stubborn, Gin. You were fucking attacked last night."

"*I know! I was there!*" I shot back, pushing down the

fear snaking up my spine from the memory of what happened. What *could* have happened if Gideon hadn't been in the right place at the right time.

"Look around you." He gestured at his luxurious home. "This place has everything you need. A gorgeous view. A pool. There's even a workout room. It's only a short drive to the beach. There's much more space than in that tiny townhouse you're living in now."

"I like my townhouse. It has everything I need. I'm just one person."

"Your mom thinks it's a good idea, too," he added somewhat guardedly.

"You talked to my mother about this?" I slammed my mug onto the kitchen island.

"Of course, I did. She cares about you. Wants you to be safe. And you'll be safe here with round-the-clock security."

My blood boiling, I spun from him and stomped farther into the kitchen, flinging open various cabinets.

"What are you looking for?"

"Flour. Vanilla. Sugar." I threw up my hands in irritation. "Shit to bake with."

"What are you in the mood for? I'll have Elena make whatever you want."

I faced him and glowered, my annoyance growing by the second. "If you want to live to see tomorrow, William Joseph Pierce, you'll let me bake."

I wasn't sure if it was the look I gave him or the fact I used his full name that made him back off. Thankfully, he got the hint, giving me space as I carried a bunch of ingredients from the pantry and set them on the kitchen island. Opening one of the oversized drawers, I found a bunch of mixing bowls, along with spatulas of various sizes.

Most people worked out when they were stressed. Or had a drink.

I baked. It was something I'd picked up from my mother. Whenever I'd had a bad day, she dragged me into the kitchen and we baked together. Something about the precise measurements needed helped me focus on something else.

Plus, the end result was always delicious.

But I wasn't sure even my favorite cupcakes would make me less irritated with Liam.

"I'm sorry, Gin." He approached me cautiously as I measured the ingredients I'd need for my snickerdoodle cupcakes. "I thought... I thought you'd want her to know. She's your mother."

I slammed the spatula onto the counter, flour flying everywhere.

"And I planned on telling her. *Myself*. Without you going behind my back and using this as a way to con me into moving in with you. I came out here to finally live my own life. To figure out who I am. And I can't do that if you're constantly trying to take care of me. I can take care of myself, Liam!"

My voice echoed in the vast space, my muscles tensing. I took several deep breaths to control my anger, then focused my eyes on his.

"You may not get it," I said firmly. "May not understand why this is so important to me. But I need to be on my own right now. I went to undergrad just a few miles away from where I grew up. Same with grad school. I even did my doctoral program in Atlanta. I'm finally on my own. I was *supposed* to be on my own, anyway, before you went and bought this place." I waved my hand around. "While I appreciate you wanting to be here for me, I need to do this. Need to move on from...everything. So please. Let me have this."

Several moments of tense silence ticked by as Liam stared at me. Finally, he pushed out a long sigh and enveloped me in his arms, kissing the top of my head.

"I'm sorry, Gin," he soothed. "I'm trying not to be so overprotective. It's just..." He pinched his lips together. "I can't stand the idea of losing you. Of something happening to you like—"

"And you won't," I cut him off before he could utter Samuel's name. Sometimes I wondered if he would have been this upset over losing Samuel if he knew we'd been seeing each other behind his back.

"But you need to let me live my life. You do that and you won't lose me."

"Promise?"

"Of course." I hoisted myself onto my toes and pressed a chaste kiss to his cheek, quickly pulling back before he could see it for anything more than a friendly kiss. "You know I adore your stubborn ass." I threw a wink his way as I returned to the mixing bowl.

"And I love you. No matter how crazy you make me sometimes."

CHAPTER TEN

Gideon

I sipped on my coffee, enjoying the tranquil stillness of the predawn hours as I sat outside The Daily Grind on Monday morning. The world was just beginning to wake up, and I relished in the peaceful solitude.

Until the sound of a dog barking cut through.

But not just any dog.

I knew that bark better than I knew myself these days.

I snapped my head in its direction, my heart catching in my throat as I watched a beagle mix tug Imogene along the beach, stopping every few feet to sniff whatever caught his attention.

Just like I remembered him doing whenever I took him for a walk all those years ago.

I knew Imogene had adopted him after my supposed death. Hell, I'd spent the past several months watching Imogene practically every day.

But that was from a distance.

That was no longer the case, not when Ollie's enthusiastic eyes fixated on me and he yanked Imogene toward me.

It was one thing to be close to Imogene again.

It was another to be near my old dog. My best friend. My companion.

"Ollie, slow down, boy," Imogene commanded. "What's gotten—"

She stopped short when she noticed me, remaining dumbfounded for several seconds before snapping out of her surprise.

"Oh, gosh. I'm sorry." She yanked on Ollie's leash, trying to prevent him from jumping on me. His tail wagged eagerly as he attempted to greet me with sloppy kisses and excited barks. "My dog seems to like you. And sadly, he was an obedience school dropout."

I chuckled, remembering my failed attempts to train the mutt I'd found abandoned in a cardboard box outside the gym. He was emaciated and dehydrated, and despite not having a lot of money back then, I couldn't just leave him there.

"I don't mind." I did my best to hide the emotions

bubbling to the surface over seeing my old companion. There was a time when I didn't think I ever would.

Based on the way he currently licked my face, he didn't think he'd ever see me again, either. It didn't matter that I now bore little resemblance to the man I once was. Ollie somehow knew it was me. The thought provided me with an unexpected source of comfort.

"Hey, boy." I scratched him behind his ears, remembering how much he loved that spot. His tail thumped harder against the ground, proof he still loved it just as much. "You're a happy hound, aren't you?"

Imogene studied me with curiosity, looking between Ollie and me. Would this be the tipping point? Would my dog be the thing that allowed her to put the pieces together?

"What is it?" I pressed, pushing down my nerves.

She squinted, raking her gaze over me like a detective searching for clues. A moment of tense scrutiny passed before she released a long breath and shook her head, as if reminding herself I was dead. That was the only thing that made my plan feasible. My ace card, so to speak.

No one would expect a man who was dead to suddenly re-enter their lives.

"Just trying to figure you out, Mr. Saint. That's all. You don't strike me as a dog person."

"I think there's a lot about me that might surprise you."

"I'm beginning to realize that." A blush bloomed on her cheeks as she bit her lower lip.

"Would you like to join me?" I gestured to the vacant chair across the table.

She gave me an apologetic smile. "I need to let this guy burn off some of his excess energy before he's cooped up all morning while I'm at work. He may be thirteen, but he's still a puppy at heart."

My chest squeezed at the reminder of his age. He looked to be in good shape, but I could see the evidence of his years, the normally brown fur around his eyes and nose sporting hints of white.

"You're welcome to come with us if you'd like."

I should have told her I couldn't. Came up with some excuse about needing to get home.

But when Ollie looked at me with his pleading eyes, I was powerless to resist and pulled myself to my feet, strolling alongside Imogene as Ollie led her down the beach path.

The salty breeze brushed against our skin, the sound of crashing waves creating a calming melody in the background. Imogene's hair danced in the wind, catching bits of the rising sun. As we walked, I couldn't help but admire every inch of her — the freckles sprinkled across her nose, the curve of her lips as she laughed at Ollie's antics, the hint of the tattoo visible on her hip.

And it was that tattoo that had me rethinking everything.

That and the memory of feeling her in my arms as I rushed her to the hospital.

"How are you feeling after...everything?" I asked after a few moments of comfortable silence while Ollie marked his territory, glancing back at us with a wide grin on his face, obviously proud of his accomplishment.

"Other than a few scratches and bruises, I'm fine. The doctor told me to take it easy for a few more days, hence why I'm stuck walking instead of going for a run or surfing. But I don't mind. Gives me more time with Ollie."

"You don't take him running with you?"

"He can't go super long distances. Not like he used to." She swallowed hard, a flicker of sadness washing over her expression. "Plus, he can get easily distracted, as you see," she said, her voice chipper once more. "I'd have to stop every few seconds to let him sniff, pee, or both."

As the words left her mouth, Ollie tugged her toward a nearby trash can, sniffing it for several seconds before lifting a leg and marking his territory.

"Case in point, I suppose," I said around a laugh.

"Exactly." She gave a gentle tug on Ollie's leash, and he bounded back toward us, trotting along the beach once more. "So tell me something..."

"What's that?" I took a sip of my coffee before returning my eyes to hers.

"Who are you, Gideon Saint?"

"I own a venture capital firm."

She shook her head. "Not that. I know who you are on paper. Or on the internet."

"Why, Ms. Prescott," I crooned in a light tone. "Were you Googling me over the weekend?"

A small laugh escaped her throat, and my god, the things that sound did to me.

I wished I didn't have the same reaction to her.

I wasn't *supposed* to have the same reaction to her.

But there was no denying the way every inch of me sparked to life whenever she was near.

"And if I was?" she threw back at me.

"Then I'd be lying if I said I'm not flattered by the prospect that I intrigue you."

"I'd be lying if I said you didn't. But I'm not interested in Gideon Saint, the venture capitalist."

"Oh no?"

"No. I want to know who you *really* are."

I stole a glance at her, keeping my expression as even as possible. "Who I *really* am?"

"Exactly. Things I can't find online. Like what was your first word? Or your favorite sport growing up? What made you interested in...venture capitalist-ing?"

I chuckled at the confusion on her face, her nose wrinkling.

"Or what's your favorite guilty pleasure? Who was your first love?" She hesitated, stealing a glance my way. "How were you able to snap a man's neck and not get a single scratch?" she added, somewhat cautiously.

"Does knowing I've taken a life scare you?"

She paused in her tracks and faced me. Ollie used the break to his advantage, trotting a few feet away to sniff a flip-flop that had been left on the sand.

"*Should* I be scared of you?"

"Yes." My response came without a moment's hesitation. She should have been scared of me. I *wanted* her to be scared of me.

But she didn't look at me like she was scared.

Quite the opposite.

"Is that right?" She tilted her head back, her eyes locking with mine.

"I meant what I said the other night." I swallowed hard as she inched toward me, our bodies almost touching.

This wasn't supposed to happen. My pulse shouldn't have been racing. My erection shouldn't have been straining against my pants. My mind shouldn't have been fantasizing about crushing my lips against hers.

But as she drew closer, all I could think about was

whether she still tasted of sugar, vanilla, and something uniquely Imogene.

"I'm not a hero," I reminded her in a husky voice.

"I know what you said. But that still doesn't change the fact that you don't scare me. I can see you for what you really are."

"And what's that?" My mouth inched toward hers of its own volition.

"You're..."

"Yes?" Raw hunger expanded inside me as I drifted my gaze over her features in a heated caress.

I went into this plan with the intention of getting close to Imogene. After all, I wanted Liam to know how it felt to lose everything important to him, Imogene included.

I just didn't realize it would be this difficult. I thought I'd be stronger. That I'd remember her for what she was to me. A tool. Nothing else.

Because right now, as she cupped my cheek, she felt like so much more than someone I planned to use, then toss aside.

She felt real.

I felt real.

"You're...," she said again, her chest rising and falling in a quicker rhythm.

"Yes," I exhaled as I framed her face with my hands, my fingers digging into her hair.

"You're—"

A sharp tug around my legs forced me to drop my hold on her, both of us snapping our eyes to our feet, Ollie's leash now wrapped tightly around us.

While that wasn't disastrous in and of itself, that was the precise moment a seagull swooped in front of Ollie.

In the seconds before he had a chance to charge, instinct took over and I barked out, *"Ollie! Heel!"* at the same time as Imogene shouted the same command.

Her body tensed as her widened eyes locked onto mine, suspicion swirling within. "How did you—"

"I guess he knows some commands after all," I responded, stepping out of Ollie's trap as he sat at Imogene's side, waiting for the treat he knew would follow upon successfully obeying a command.

Imogene reached into her pocket and held out her palm, but her gaze remained fixed on me, the crease in her brow growing by the second.

"How did you know he'd listen to *that* command?"

"I grew up around a lot of dogs." I shrugged nonchalantly, praying she'd buy my story. "It's one of the first commands you try to teach."

Silence hung heavy in the air for what felt like an eternity before she let out a long sigh and broke her gaze from mine.

"Of course. Right." She untangled Ollie's leash and held it taut, increasing the distance between us. "I should get home and feed this guy his breakfast." She averted her gaze, pushing a few wayward tendrils of hair behind her ear. " You'd think he hasn't been fed in days the way he acts if I'm even a minute late."

I nodded, remembering that all too well. "I won't keep you. I'm just glad to see you out and about."

She studied me for several protracted moments, then spun, tugging a reluctant Ollie along with her.

After a few feet, she paused, glancing over her shoulder, her analytical gaze sweeping over me once more. Luckily, it only lasted a second before she continued on her way.

CHAPTER ELEVEN

Imogene

I sat on the floor of my office Saturday morning surrounded by boxes, doing my best to finally unpack my life. Maybe if Liam saw my townhouse actually looked lived in instead of being a collection of unpacked boxes and makeshift furniture, he'd stop pestering me to move in.

Going through these boxes also helped me take my mind off my conflicted feelings about Gideon.

I hadn't been able to stop thinking about him all week. About the way his voice thundered the command for Ollie to heel.

It stole my breath.

Brought me back in time.

He sounded so much like Samuel. If I didn't know better, I would have thought he was there with me.

But that was impossible.

Samuel Tate died five years ago. A fact I kept reminding myself of more and more since I first met Gideon Saint. I went through this very thing around the anniversary of his death every year. It was natural to think about him more. That was all this was. A natural part of the grieving process.

Except I still seemed to be stuck in denial.

Ollie pushed his wet snout against my hand, and I scratched him behind his ears.

"I know, pal. I'm crazy."

He whimpered, lowering himself onto the floor and looking up at me with those sad eyes.

"You miss him, too, don't you?"

He inched forward, resting his chin on my lap as I continued unpacking photos and knickknacks to decorate the built-in bookshelves in my office. There were photos of Mama, Lachlan, and me on their wedding day. Some of Lachlan and me bobbing up and down on our surfboards in Hawaii, solving the problems of the world, as he put it. Photos from all my various graduations — high school, college, graduate school.

Mixed in with these memories were pictures of Melanie and me throughout the years. In the beginning, it was just us. But as time went on, Liam started appearing in some of the photos. It wasn't long before Samuel came into the picture, too.

Pulling out a selfie of Samuel, Ollie, and me on the beach in Hilton Head, I ran my finger along the image, drinking in his striking blue eyes. If he had higher cheekbones and more angular features, as well as stubble along his jawline, I could see the resemblance to Gideon. They were around the same height, although Gideon was certainly more built. Not that Samuel wasn't in great shape. He was. He was skilled at wrestling and martial arts, even if that had simply become a hobby once the company he started with Liam took off.

I placed the frame on a shelf, my gaze lingering on it for several long moments before I returned to my task. After unwrapping a few more frames and setting them on the shelves, I pulled out a keepsake box.

When I lifted the lid, I sucked in a quick breath at the sight of all the letters Samuel had written to me during our relationship. It was one of the things I loved about him. Loved how he took the time to put pen to paper and write down his thoughts and feelings. Now, these letters were the only piece of Samuel Tate I had left.

Besides Ollie, of course.

With a nostalgic smile, I pulled a letter from the box and unfolded the slightly warn paper, Samuel's familiar scrawl greeting me. I often joked about getting him a penmanship workbook since I could barely read his handwriting. Now, I relished in his chicken scratch.

My Dearest Imogene,

I love watching you sleep.

That's not too creepy, is it? There's just something about admiring your chest rise and fall, the look of peace on your face that I'll never get tired of. It's one of my favorite looks on you.

I'll let you take a wild guess what my other favorite look on you is.

You may be lying next to me, but I didn't want to waste the opportunity to let you know just how important you are to me. I never want to waste an opportunity where you're concerned. I'll always tell you how happy you make me. How grateful I am to have you in my life, regardless of the complications.

How much I love you.

Completely.

Totally.

Unconditionally.

Yours forever,

Samuel

"Unconditionally," I repeated, tracing the symbol of unconditional love he sketched beside his name.

The same symbol that was now tattooed on my hip in the exact place he often mindlessly traced when we lay in bed together.

A sudden chiming from my cell pierced through the silence, and Ollie jumped up and ran out of the office, growling and barking at the front door. It didn't matter that a doorbell didn't ring.

Since Liam sent someone to install my smart doorbell earlier in the week, Ollie figured out the exact sound my phone made whenever someone was at the door.

"Settle, Ollie," I called out, pulling myself to my feet. "It's probably just Auntie Mel." I unlocked my phone and navigated to the doorbell app, pulling up the feed.

When my eyes fell on a man in a courier uniform holding an oversized box instead of a tall brunette, I paused in my tracks.

A hint of trepidation trickled down my spine at the possibility it might be another necklace, but I quickly brushed it off. I couldn't have this reaction anytime I received a delivery. Not at the rate at which I ordered things online.

Hushing Ollie, I walked toward the front door and opened it.

"Imogene Prescott?" the courier asked.

"Yes."

"Sign here." He handed me a clipboard and pointed to a line with an X.

I did as he instructed, making sure to memorize the name on his shirt, as well as any distinguishing features in his appearance, like the cleft in his chin and wide set of his dark eyes. I had a feeling it wasn't necessary, though. He made no attempt to hide his face from the doorbell camera.

Once I returned his clipboard, he handed me the package.

"Have a nice day." He headed toward his idling truck just as Melanie pulled her car into the driveway.

She didn't waste a second, making a beeline toward me, her concerned eyes focused on the box in my hands.

"What is that, Imogene?"

"I don't know."

She followed me into my townhouse, closing the door as I set the box on the coffee table.

"You don't think it's—"

"It's not from my mother's bakery."

"Not sure that makes much of a difference." She dropped her bag onto the floor and bent to scratch Ollie's head.

As well as sneak him a few treats.

"It's way too heavy for a necklace." I squinted, noticing a faint logo on the corner. "Looks like it's from Alchemy, that dress store I went to a few days ago."

"Is it now?" Her concern slowly waning, she moved to the couch and plopped down, patting the cushion for me to join her. Instead, Ollie jumped up, licking Melanie's face. "At least I'm getting *some* action, even if it's from a dog." She rubbed her nose against Ollie's. "But that's okay. Because dogs are infinitely better than humans. Aren't they, Ollie?"

He barked in agreement.

"Happy Birthday, by the way," she said as I sat on the other side of Ollie.

"Thanks, Mel."

"Now open this." She bounced in her seat. "Not going to lie, Gin. I'm kind of excited to see what's in it."

I bit my bottom lip. "Me, too."

I pulled the red ribbon and the elaborate bow came undone. When I lifted the lid, I found a note with an appointment card for an upscale spa in San Diego attached to it.

"Looks like we're going to the spa today," I told Melanie, showing her the card.

"Thank god." She relaxed into the couch. "I've been meaning to schedule a massage. Now we get to do it on someone else's dime." She nodded toward the note. "What else does it say?"

I unfolded the paper and scanned the masculine scrawl. A feeling of déjà vu careened into me, making me breathless. It wasn't *his* handwriting. For one, I could actually read it. But it reminded me of the last birthday I celebrated with Samuel. How he'd sent a courier to my apartment with the first clue to a scavenger hunt he'd planned just for me.

It was a birthday I'd never forget.

"A driver will pick you up at one o'clock to take you and a guest to your appointments," I read out loud. "Enjoy your day. You deserve it. Happy birthday, Imogene."

"Any indication of who your secret admirer is?" Melanie leaned over my shoulder to read the note for herself.

I shrugged dismissively. "Probably just Liam."

Although, I had serious doubts about whether Liam would have done something like this. He wasn't the type of person to book a spa day. Not to mention, he didn't call me Imogene.

"Probably," Melanie agreed unconvincingly. "What does it say on the bottom?"

She'd obviously already read it. She simply wanted me to read it out loud.

"Please wear this tonight," I continued. "While I find you absolutely beautiful even in a pair of yoga pants and t-shirt, the second I saw this dress, I knew there was only one body it deserved to be on."

"Yup. It's *definitely* from Liam." She rolled her eyes, her skepticism loud and clear.

I tried to reel in my excitement over the idea of some mysterious admirer not only arranging a day of pampering with my best friend, but also buying me a new dress to wear. It was a losing battle, though, especially since I could only think of one person who might do something like this for me.

Or maybe I just *wanted* him to be the one to do all of this for me.

Pulling back the tissue, I released a gasp when I saw the stunning champagne dress adorned with crystals that shimmered in the light. I rose to my feet and lifted it out of the box, holding it up to my body as I looked at my reflection in the floor-length mirror hanging on the far wall.

"Is that?" Melanie began.

"It is," I exhaled, my mind reeling.

"How?"

"I don't know."

I'd been looking at this very dress a few days ago, but baulked at the price tag. Instead, I ended up buying a little black dress at a bargain store.

Yet someone knew I'd fawned over this dress, especially after the sales girl encouraged me to try it on. The second I did, I regretted it. I loved everything about the dress, from the off-the-shoulder sleeves, to the plunging neckline, to the way it hugged my body, to the asymmetric hem that made my legs feel like they went on for miles.

Wearing it had made me feel beautiful.

So much so that I'd texted Melanie a photo of me in it and demanded she stage an immediate intervention so I didn't spend my rent money on a dress I'd only wear once.

Being the good friend she was, she told me I deserved it, but also respected how financially responsible I was trying to be.

The last thing I expected was for someone to buy it for me.

"I guess Liam really wants you to have the best birthday ever." Melanie's tone was borderline antagonizing.

"I guess so," I murmured, still dumbfounded.

A part of me wanted to believe this was all Liam. It would have made more sense. I'd agreed to turn on location sharing on my phone so he wouldn't worry about me when he was out of town. He could have easily seen I was shopping for a dress, then called the store and ordered it.

But that wasn't his handwriting on the card.

I had a feeling I already knew who sent this.

And the only way he could have known about this dress was if he'd been watching me.

The idea should have unsettled me.

Instead, I couldn't control the swarm of butterflies that took flight in my stomach over the prospect.

CHAPTER TWELVE

Imogene

"This is heaven," Melanie exhaled, sipping on a glass of champagne while she sat in the pedicure chair beside me, both of us clad in robes with the spa's insignia on it. We'd spent the past few hours being pampered with one of the best massages I'd ever had.

"I'll drink to that." I tilted my glass toward hers and we clinked them together before taking a sip of the smooth champagne.

"Just make sure I don't leave tonight without thanking Liam." She smirked.

Over the course of our afternoon, she'd brought up Liam several times, mentioning how thoughtful he was to organize all of this for my birthday. Each time, I sensed she only did so in an attempt to get me to share who *really* could have been behind it all.

So far, I hadn't.

That was the thing about spending hours being pampered, though. It gave me time to think.

And the more I thought about Gideon Saint, the more I felt the urge to confide in someone about him.

"We both know Liam didn't arrange any of this," I told her over the top of my champagne flute.

"Finally!" Her voice echoed through the calm serenity, the only other sound that of the ambient music and a nearby fountain. "I thought I was going to have to torture the truth out of you."

"Why were you so quick to assume it wasn't him? It could have been."

"Don't get me wrong. I love Liam, but he's not the most thoughtful person. It's not that he doesn't care," she added quickly. "But booking an appointment at *the* premier spa in San Diego so you can have a relaxing birthday, as well as sending you a dress to wear for your party? And not just any dress, but the dress you were foaming at your mouth over? That's not something Liam would do. Not something he'd even *think* about doing. I mean, how many designer purses are you up to now?"

I blew out a soft laugh. My closet was filled with bags of various sizes, all thanks to Liam. That, and overpriced shoes. Apparently, he was under the impression I was like the women on *Sex and the City* and only cared about expensive purses and shoes. Not that there was anything wrong with that.

I just wasn't really a purse and high heel kind of girl. My work uniform consisted of a polo shirt, yoga pants, and sneakers. The only times I dressed up over the past year had been whenever Liam was in town and asked me to attend some business dinner or charity gala with him. Or when going out for a night on the town with Melanie.

"Which begs the question of *who* arranged all of this for you." She leaned closer and dropped her voice. "Perhaps a mysterious man who can snap a guy's neck in one move."

I lifted my glass back to my mouth, hoping to hide my smile at the thought of Gideon, but it was impossible.

"I'm right, aren't I? There's something going on between you and Gideon."

"Not...exactly."

Melanie's eyes lit up with excitement. "Then tell me *exactly* what is going on."

On a long sigh, I took another sip of my champagne. Then I settled into the chair and told my best friend about my various encounters with Gideon, starting with that first morning and going into detail about each of our subsequent encounters, ending with Monday morning.

"Okay. So you keep running into each other and he saved your life. What aren't you telling me?"

I worried my bottom lip. I could very well lie, insist I wasn't keeping anything from her. But Melanie knew me better than anyone. She already sensed I wasn't being completely forthcoming. If there was anyone I could tell my concerns without judgment, it was Melanie.

"Have you noticed something...unusual about his eyes?"

Melanie tilted her head, her brow creasing with confusion. "Unusual? I don't—"

"The color. The shape."

It took a moment for her to register what I was referring to.

"They remind you of Sam," she breathed.

"A little." My expression faltered as I pushed down the lump building in my throat. "And then Monday, he told Ollie to heel."

"What? Say it isn't so," she responded sarcastically. "I'll alert the media. Prepare a press release. He told a dog to heel?"

"That's not what I mean." I placed my hand over hers. "It was *how* he said it, Mel. He sounded so much like Samuel." I fought against the tremble in my voice. "If I hadn't been looking at this man whose face didn't resemble his, I would have thought he was there with me."

Melanie's expression softened as she studied me

intently, seeming to weigh my words and find understanding. Finally, she pushed out a deep sigh.

"You just said it yourself, Gin. His face doesn't resemble Sam's. I can understand why it might spark some memories. He does crossword puzzles. Ollie seemed to take to him quickly. But we both read the police report. Based on the amount of blood found in his car—"

"I know. I just..." I shook my head, struggling to find the words to explain what was going through my brain.

Hell, *I* didn't even know what was going through my brain.

"He makes you feel things, doesn't he?"

"It sounds crazy. I know next to nothing about him."

"You don't have to know his full history to have chemistry. And based on what I saw the other night in the hospital room, the two of you had it in spades. He could barely take his eyes off you." She leaned closer. "And don't forget the lengths he went to in order to keep you safe. He snapped a guy's neck, for crying out loud. He could have been arrested if the detective hadn't decided against pressing charges. That's worth a thank-you fuck, if you ask me."

I nearly choked on my champagne. "Jesus, Mel. Warn me before you say something like that."

She shrugged. "At this point, you should be used to it. I don't have much of a brain-to-mouth filter."

"It's one of the things I love about you. But I'm not going to have sex with him as a thank you for saving my life."

"Then have sex with him for you. I'm sure you've thought about it."

She was right. I *had* thought about what it might be like to be with Gideon. Probably *too* much. The feel of his arms around me. The heat of his breath. The roughness of his unshaven jawline against my skin.

Was I ready to go there with another person. It was one thing to sleep with Liam. There was no spark. No connection.

Gideon was different.

"I just..." I pushed out a breath. "I can't."

"Why?" Melanie pressed. "And I swear to god, if you bring up Liam again, I'm going to scream. I adore him. And you. But you know how I feel about the idea of the two of you." She gave me a knowing look, her disapproval evident. "I still think he took advantage of you after Sam died."

"He didn't know about Samuel," I reminded her. "Still doesn't. You're the only one who knew the truth about our relationship."

"Even so, it was obvious you were hurting after his death. I get wanting to offer you comfort. But there's a way to do that without taking advantage of you, like Liam did."

I understood why she might have felt that way. But I *was* a willing participant.

Was it unhealthy? Absolutely.

But on those days when I didn't think anything would make the hurt of Samuel's death go away, Liam gave me what I needed. An escape from the crippling void that consumed me.

"We took advantage of each other."

"Further proof it's toxic."

"I knew he was safe. Knew I wouldn't get attached and end up broken hearted."

"What about Liam, though?"

"What do you mean?"

She narrowed her gaze on me. "You know how he feels about you."

"We haven't hooked up in over a year. We agreed our friendship was too important to ruin."

"I guarantee he'd drop everything if you told him you changed your mind. If you returned even a fraction of the feelings he's always had for you."

"All the more reason I shouldn't pursue anything with Gideon. I don't want to hurt Liam."

"Do you even hear yourself, Ginny? You've met a guy you're interested in for the first time since losing Sam and you're not going to pursue it because of how Liam might react? Don't let him manipulate you. Don't let him *control* you."

"He's not—"

"Answer me this," she interjected. "If Liam weren't in the picture, what would you do about Gideon? Better yet. What would you have done differently with Sam?"

I parted my lips, wanting to insist I wouldn't have done anything differently. But I couldn't lie to her.

There were so many things I would have changed if I didn't have to worry about hurting Liam. I certainly wouldn't have kept my relationship with Samuel a secret. Wouldn't have snuck around like we did.

"Don't let Liam stand in your way again," Melanie encouraged when I didn't immediately respond. She covered my hand with hers and squeezed. "If losing Samuel taught you anything, it's that tomorrow isn't promised. That it's important to live with no regrets."

I swallowed hard, pushing down the emotions welling inside of me.

I had more than my fair share of regrets when it came to Samuel. Especially the fact that we'd fought the last time we saw each other. He was done loving me in the shadows. Was ready to tell Liam everything.

But I was a coward.

Like Melanie, Samuel had accused me of allowing Liam to manipulate me. Of letting my misplaced guilt control me.

Because of that, Samuel went to his grave questioning my love and devotion.

"No regrets," I said.

"No regrets," Melanie repeated, her eyes awash with sincerity. Then her expression turned conniving. "And I think you should start this regret-free life by giving yourself the birthday gift of some ridiculously hot sex with a ridiculously sexy man."

"Sex doesn't solve everything," I reminded her.

"No. But it sure does make things feel better, even if for a minute."

I blew out a laugh. "I can't argue with that."

CHAPTER THIRTEEN

Gideon

I navigated my car past the gated entrance of Liam's sprawling estate and along the cobblestone driveway lined with perfectly manicured greens. The instant I pulled to a stop in front of his palatial home, a valet approached and opened the door of my Jaguar convertible.

After handing him the keys, I started toward the entrance, pushing down any lingering reservations about tonight.

Nothing could go wrong. I couldn't waste this unexpected opportunity. I needed to stay in control. Needed to keep my hatred toward these people far below the surface.

This would be vastly different from the past few

times I'd purposefully ran into Imogene. In mere minutes, I'd be in a room surrounded by dozens of people I once knew in my old life as Samuel Tate.

People who betrayed me.

Who conspired to kill me.

I couldn't do anything that would make them suspicious. Instead, I needed to become one of them.

I was the Trojan Horse, and they'd unknowingly allowed me inside the city gates.

Fixing my expression, I smoothed a hand down my suit jacket as I ascended the steps. The door immediately swung open and a man in a crisp tuxedo welcomed me.

He ushered me through the opulent foyer and into a high-ceilinged living area where a crystal chandelier sparkled overhead and marble floors gleamed beneath my feet.

On the back patio, I was met with even more extravagance — elegantly dressed guests lingered by dozens of high-top tables, strings of party lights dangling overhead, a jazz quartet filling the air with smooth melodies.

But what caught my attention was the breathtaking view from this vantage point in the San Diego hills — miles and miles of ocean stretching out before us, the vast expanse sparkling in the moonlight.

My gaze swept across the buzzing crowd, taking inventory of everyone I recognized.

Everyone I once considered a friend.

Not anymore.

It didn't take long for me to find Imogene, even in a sea of people. She stood out, her shimmering beauty drawing my attention like a moth to a flame. Especially in that dress.

When I first I saw her in it earlier in the week, I knew she deserved to have it.

I tried to convince myself the only reason I bought it and treated her and Melanie to a day at the spa was to endear Imogene to me even more.

To piss off Liam even more.

Deep down, there was a part of me that did it because of the look of pure happiness I observed on her face as she admired herself in the mirror that day in the store.

Also because she looked absolutely gorgeous in the dress, her blonde hair falling in gentle waves to her mid back.

But what had my cock straining against my pants tonight was the sight of her crimson lips. As sexy as they were, they were a fucking inconvenience. I was here for one reason, and one reason only.

Revenge.

I needed to remember that.

Squaring my shoulders, I confidently started across the patio, transitioning into the charming and charismatic man I needed to be in order to earn favor with these people.

I only made it a few steps before Liam approached, an expression of forced congeniality plastered on his face.

"Mr. Saint…" He extended his hand toward me, playing the part of the gracious host. "So glad you could make it."

I mirrored his enthusiasm, acting as if we were old friends.

Little did he know we once were.

"I appreciate the invitation."

"Not at all." He patted my back, steering me toward a group of well-dressed men. "There are a few people I'd like you to meet. You may recognize Jimmy here from his recent senatorial campaign." He gestured at the man of average height and build, his blonde hair slicked back, a carefully crafted smile painted on his face.

"Senator Turner." I offered him my hand. "It's a pleasure."

James Mitchell Turner had come a long way from the district attorney he was just a few years ago. Now he was a U.S. Senator with his eyes on a possible presidential run in the next election.

Paid for in part with bribe money he'd received from Liam to make sure the man they'd accused of murdering me never got his day in court. He'd used his position and influence as a prosecutor to approve plea deals for several defendants awaiting trial on various drug-related offenses. In exchange, these inmates agreed to attack Jonah while he was being held without bail.

Jonah wasn't the first inmate James Turner helped silence, either. Nor was he the last.

"And this man here is the only person I trust to manage my investments, Alton Sinclair."

"Is that right?"

Since the last time I'd seen him, he'd definitely put on some weight and lost a bit of hair, his formerly full head of dark hair now receding.

"I'm in the market for a new financial advisor."

"And you are?" He arched a bushy brow as we shook hands.

"This is Gideon Saint," Liam explained. "He helped Ginny last weekend. He's also the CEO of Growth Ventures."

As expected, Alton's interest in me immediately piqued, probably seeing dollar signs in his eyes.

"I'd hate to think what could have happened if you hadn't been there to help her," James said somberly, always the politician.

"We all do," Liam offered on a hard swallow.

"I'm glad I could be of assistance." I gave them a tight smile. "Speaking of which, I'd like to say a quick hello to the guest of honor. If you'll excuse me, gentlemen." I started to turn, not wanting to be around them any longer than necessary, especially since none of them seemed remotely suspicious about who I was.

I wanted to keep it that way, not overplay my hand just yet.

"Come find me later on," Alton suggested, making me stop in my tracks. "We'll discuss how I can make you even richer than you already are." He raised a glass to his lips and sipped on the amber liquid.

"I prefer not to mix business and pleasure," I replied so as to not sound too eager.

Even though this was exactly why I didn't hesitate to accept Liam's invitation to come tonight. Becoming part of their world was necessary for me to destroy them.

And that started with Alton Sinclair.

He would be the first domino to fall, setting off a chain reaction that would lead to their downfall.

"Ah, a man with boundaries. I admire that."

"Otherwise, I'd work all the time." I reached into the inside pocket of my suit jacket and handed him a business card. "Have your assistant call mine. Maybe we can arrange a meeting this week."

"I have some business up in San Francisco, but perhaps we can talk at the tournament if you're going."

"Tournament?" I cocked a brow, feigning ignorance.

"I host a charity golf tournament every year up in Pebble Beach," Liam explained. "It benefits a youth program a friend of ours started before he died. He may be gone, but I wanted to do something to honor his memory."

"That sounds admirable."

It took every ounce of resolve I had not to tackle Liam to the ground and wrap my hands around his throat. I knew the truth. He didn't give a shit about honoring my memory.

He was simply using my death for publicity purposes.

"You should join us," Alton suggested. "We just had a guy in our foursome back out. It's for a good cause and gets you a tax write off."

Liam darted him a warning look, but it was obvious Alton was thinking of one thing only. Getting his hands on my money.

It was nice to know some things hadn't changed.

"I'd be delighted." My lips curved up in the corners. All the chips were falling into place even better than I'd expected. "Now, if you'll excuse me."

I retreated from them and moved through the crowd toward the table where I'd spied Imogene minutes earlier. Luckily, she was still there, Melanie at her side. Despite the hundred or so people here, they seemed to be in their own little world, not caring to interact with any of Liam's guests, apart from a few polite exchanges.

As I neared them, Melanie gently nudged Imogene.

She darted her head in my direction, her eyes locking with mine.

My god, she looked stunning. I noticed her the second I walked onto the patio, but being this close, seeing those red lips part, her chest heaving, I fought to resist the temptation to slam my mouth against hers. Find out if she still tasted like I remembered.

Find out if she still kissed like I remembered.

Throw her against the wall and fuck every last remnant of Liam from her body.

Bonus points if it happened when he was in earshot.

"Ms. Prescott," I greeted, struggling to keep my eyes locked on hers instead of ogling her body.

"Mr. Saint."

"Happy birthday." I curved toward her and pressed a soft kiss to her cheek. Instead of pulling back right away, I lingered, inhaling her delicious scent. Coconut. Pineapple. And fresh air.

Exactly as I remembered.

"You're stunning," I murmured, my voice husky and low.

Her shoulders rose and fell, her breathing increasing with every second I remained within a whisper of her.

She always wore her desire well. It was one of the things I loved about her. When we were alone, she didn't hold back. Always let me see how much she craved me.

Let me know how desperate she was for me.

In those moments, I was confident I saw the real Imogene. Not the person she pretended to be around everyone else.

Much like she did now as she put space between us, nervously scanning the crowd for Liam.

"You remember Melanie, don't you?" Imogene said, then frowned. "I'm not sure I introduced you two the other night."

"You didn't," Melanie interjected. "But I did." She extended her hand toward me. "Pleasure to see you again, Gideon."

"Likewise." I turned my attention back on Imogene. "Have you been enjoying your birthday?"

"I have actually." She pursed her lips together. "I received a surprise gift this morning, treating both Melanie and me to an afternoon at the spa. In addition to this dress."

She did a quick twirl, and it took everything I had to refrain from yanking her against me. But I remained cool and detached.

"Whoever sent it to you has good taste."

"I'll drink to that." Melanie gave me a conniving look, then raised her flute toward me before taking a sip.

"Sorry to interrupt," Liam cut through, appearing from out of nowhere. "I need to steal the birthday girl for a few moments." He snaked an arm around Imogene's waist and yanked her against him.

I wanted to break that arm.

Hell, I wanted to do so much more than that. I reminded myself he'd get what was coming to him.

"Right now?" Imogene stepped out of his hold.

"I only need five minutes. All these people are here for you," he said in a tone that bordered on being conde-scending.

"Right. Of course." She set her champagne flute onto the table and met my gaze. "I'm sorry. I won't be long."

"No apologies necessary."

With a fabricated smile, Liam ushered her toward a group of people I doubted she had anything in common with.

The entire time, he kept his hand firmly planted on her hip.

But that wasn't what struck me as odd.

It was the way she tried to get away from him.

He wouldn't let her, though, keeping his hand glued to her.

"A little tip for you."

"What's that?" I turned my attention toward Melanie, mindful to keep Imogene in my peripheral vision.

I didn't trust Liam before I learned he was behind those necklaces and the attack.

Now, I *really* didn't.

"Maybe tone down the flaring nostrils and

clenching fists," Melanie said softly. "It's a dead give-away you'd love nothing more than to rip him apart from limb to limb." She pulled back, her voice brightening. "Drink?"

"I could certainly use one."

She spun on her heels, walking the short distance toward the bar, and I followed. "What would you like? My treat." She winked.

"Scotch. Neat."

"Manhattan for me," she told the bartender, who got to work on our drinks.

"So what's the deal with them?" I gestured toward Liam.

I already knew what the deal with them was, but I needed to act as if I'd just met them mere days ago, especially around Melanie. A twinge of guilt settled in my stomach over the idea that I wasn't just deceiving Imogene, but also Melanie.

She was truly innocent in all of this.

Although lately, I'd been having doubts about Imogene, too. Maybe she hadn't betrayed me like I originally thought.

Maybe she hadn't forgotten about me.

"It's complicated."

Melanie thanked the bartender as he handed us our drinks. Then we returned to the table.

"Gin's has always felt a sort of responsibility to Liam.

His mother was killed when he was ten. The victim of a serial killer."

"I'm sorry to hear that," I responded, feigning compassion.

"I assume you know who Imogene is. Her…background."

I kept my expression even. "What makes you say that?"

"You somehow knew she all but salivated over the dress she's currently wearing and sent it to her. Call me crazy, but I don't think it was a coincidence." She gave me a pointed stare.

"And what makes you think I was the one who sent it?"

"There was a note wishing her a happy birthday. Wishing *Imogene* a happy birthday. And since you're the only one who calls her Imogene…"

I studied her for a beat, then pushed out a breath, knowing full well she wouldn't let this go. Melanie Burnham was nothing if not tenacious.

"I've had a few guards following her from a distance," I confessed, then quickly added, "but only this week. I wanted to make sure she was safe. That's all."

I didn't tell her the person I was trying to protect Imogene from was currently parading her around the patio like she was yet another one of his prized possessions.

"I can only assume if you'd go to that much trouble, you probably also ran a background check and learned precisely who her sperm donor is."

I nodded subtly.

"Well, he killed Liam's mom. As part of coming to terms with who she was, Imogene reached out to all of her father's victims, Liam included."

"And they became friends?"

She pinched her lips together in contemplation. "I think they gave each other what the other was looking for."

"And what's that?"

"Answers. Understanding. Forgiveness."

"I see." I brought my glass to my lips and took a long sip, my gaze focused on Imogene.

"I understand that Liam can be a bit...intense. And sometimes Imogene acts the way she does because she feels a certain level of responsibility to him. Or maybe guilt. Take this party, for example." She waved her hand at our surroundings. "If it were up to her, she'd spend her birthday on her surfboard. Or holed up in some cabin with no electricity or cell service where no one could find her. She doesn't need all of this."

"But she puts up with it to make Liam happy."

"More or less."

"What about making herself happy?"

"That's the million dollar question, one I've asked

her quite a lot. I think part of the problem is she lost someone who made her extremely happy. Since then, she's just been going through the motions." She lifted her eyes to mine. "Until recently. And I have a feeling you might have something to do with that, Mr. Saint."

She cracked a smile before her expression turned severe.

"But if you hurt her, I will make your life a living hell. My father's a retired Navy SEAL. He knows how to kill people and make sure their bodies are never found. I'd hate to use his expertise on you."

I laughed, hoping she didn't pick up on my nerves.

Because the truth was, I'd already hurt Imogene.

She just didn't realize it yet.

CHAPTER FOURTEEN

Imogene

I ran my fingertips along the smooth, worn spines of the books filling one of the shelves in Liam's library. Since he knew how much I loved being surrounded by the smell of books and leather, he made sure each of his homes had a quiet space just for me.

I once told him it wasn't necessary to go through all the trouble.

He'd replied by saying it worked for the Beast and he hoped it might work for him one day.

He'd failed to take into account the explosive chemistry between Belle and the Beast. Even when she despised him, there was still a connection she couldn't ignore.

That wasn't the case with Liam and me. There was

no deep connection. No intense attraction. No powerful reaction to a single look, word, touch.

Not like there was with Samuel.

And lately, with Gideon.

In fact, Gideon was one of the reasons I sought refuge inside the library, despite the party still going on outside. It wasn't just to have a reprieve from pretending I actually liked all the people Liam had invited. Instead, it was to have a break from the heat that radiated through my body every time my eyes met Gideon's.

And they seemed to meet often, two magnets drawn to each other in an inexplicable and mysterious way.

When the deep, confident thud of masculine footsteps echoed from the hallway, coming to a stop in the doorway, I groaned, certain it was Liam here to drag me back to the party.

"I'll be out soon," I said sweetly, not turning to face him. "Just wanted a few minutes to myself."

"My apologies," a voice responded.

But it wasn't Liam's.

I whirled around, my breath catching in my throat at the sight of Gideon standing in the doorway. My pulse kicked up as I drank in his striking features — dark hair that was slightly disheveled, a hint of scruff along his jawline, and a black suit that hugged his muscular frame perfectly.

It didn't help that Liam seemed to deliberately keep

me away from Gideon most of the night. Still, I couldn't stop seeking him out in the crowd.

Couldn't stop focusing on his lips.

Couldn't stop remembering how they felt on my skin.

Couldn't stop fantasizing about how they'd feel on other parts of my body.

If a gentle kiss to my cheek unhinged me, I could only imagine how I'd respond if he kissed me for real.

I imagined he kissed with authority. With control. With determination. He wouldn't be gentle or timid. No. He'd be possessive, stealing my kiss with the ruthless efficiency of a thief.

And I'd be his willing victim.

"I'll give you some privacy." He gave a subtle nod before spinning around.

"Wait," I called out.

He stopped in his tracks, his eyes meeting mine.

"You don't have to leave. I..." I blew out a breath. "I wouldn't mind some company."

He arched a single brow. "I thought you needed some time to yourself."

"More like some time away from all of them." I nodded toward the bay windows overlooking the pristine grounds.

"I take it this isn't how you pictured celebrating your

birthday." A small smile tipped on Gideon's mouth as he slowly walked toward me.

"Not in the least." I brought my wine glass to my lips and took a sip.

The intensity of his gaze held me captive, like a caged bird unable to break free.

Or perhaps, un*willing* to break free.

He leaned casually against the ornate desk in the center of the room, his dark suit clinging to every ripple and bulge of his physique. The warm glow of the subtle light cast shadows across his face, adding an air of mystery to his already intriguing presence.

"Then tell me, Imogene Prescott..." He crossed his arms over his chest, everything about him exuding power and control.

So much control.

"How would *you* prefer to spend your birthday?"

"A scavenger hunt," I answered before I could stop myself.

"A scavenger hunt?" he repeated, as if uttering words he'd never heard before.

"A few years ago, a...friend planned a scavenger hunt on my birthday." I stared into the distance as the memory danced in front of my eyes like an old movie. "That morning, a courier dropped off my first clue. And throughout the day, each clue led me to a different part of the city with a different surprise, all things he knew I'd love. Until the final clue led me..." I trailed off, my chest aching.

"Well, it doesn't matter. It was a fun, unique way to celebrate the day. Don't get me wrong," I added quickly. "I'm grateful that Liam went through the trouble of throwing this party for me."

"But you don't need all the attention."

It wasn't a question. More of a statement.

"Exactly."

"Answer me this..." He pushed off the desk, his long strides bringing him closer. "What *do* you need?"

There was a sensuality to his tone that had the tiny hairs all over my body standing on end, an electric current slowly snaking through me.

"What do I need?"

"From what I've observed, you tend to put other's needs ahead of your own. You don't like big birthday parties, yet you let your friend throw one for you."

I parted my lips, but what could I say? He wasn't wrong.

"So tell me, Imogene. What do *you* need?"

I swallowed hard, my mouth becoming dry as he continued inching toward me until there was barely any space remaining between us. His scent engulfed me in a heady mixture of leather, spice, and danger.

I sensed it from the beginning. This man was dangerous.

Yet I couldn't find it in me to care.

Not when he was the first person in years to make me feel even a fraction of what I did for Samuel.

"Or perhaps I should ask... What do you *want*?"

"I want..." My body flooded with warmth, my nerve endings lighting on fire.

"Tell me," he said again, this time more forcefully.

"I want..."

"Yes," he breathed, his lips moving even closer to mine.

My eyes fluttered into the back of my head as he looped his arm around my waist, yanking me against his body. There was no mistaking what he wanted. What he *needed*.

"I want..."

He cradled my face in his strong hands, running the pad of his thumb along my bottom lip. "Yes."

I opened my eyes and met his gaze, everything about this feeling like a dream.

Had I imagined what it might feel like to be wrapped in Gideon's arms, his body flush with mine? Of course I had, especially after my conversation with Melanie at the spa earlier today.

I didn't think I'd actually follow through with any of it. Didn't think I'd put myself out there, especially in Liam's house.

Right now, Liam was the last person on my mind.

The only thing I was thinking about was the buzz of pleasure spiraling through me, a dull ache settling in my core.

"You, Gideon." I licked my lips, my heart thrashing in my chest. "I want you."

My words echoed around us, the seconds seeming to stretch as I waited for him to do something. Say something. Anything.

But he didn't. He just stared at me, each second feeling like an eternity.

When I didn't think I could handle another moment of brutal anticipation, a groan tumbled from his throat and he tightened his grip on my head, pulling me toward him with a forceful urgency.

Then he slammed his lips against mine.

CHAPTER FIFTEEN

Imogene

Every fiber of my being screamed that this was wrong. I shouldn't have been kissing Gideon in Liam's house where he could walk in on us at any second.

But when Gideon coaxed my lips to part, his tongue sliding with mine, all thoughts of where we were and what we were doing disappeared. Instead, he was all I thought about. All I cared about.

Not Liam.

Not my past.

Just this man who invaded my every waking thought since I first saw him. His touch ignited a fire deep within me that had been dormant ever since I lost Samuel. But with Gideon's kiss, it burned brightly once more.

I moaned into him, the expert way his tongue stroked mine causing a pool of heat to surge between my legs. He tangled his fingers in my hair, his hold greedy and relentless. Everything about his kiss was exhilarating, yet familiar at the same time.

The way he held me. The way he tilted my head. The way he groaned into my mouth. I couldn't shake the feeling I'd been here before.

Maybe I had.

Maybe Gideon and I had known each other in a former life, and the powers that be sent him to help me move on from Samuel.

"Goddamn," Gideon grunted as he tore away, his chest heaving.

I'd never seen him so unhinged. So out of sorts. Up until now, he'd always maintained complete control over his emotions. Even when he took out my attacker, he did so with cold indifference.

But now, there was nothing indifferent about the way he looked at me.

His eyes blazed with intensity, his nostrils flaring with each ragged breath. His jaw clenched tightly, revealing the tension coiling through him.

With a primal growl, he slammed his lips back to mine, taking my mouth as if he owned it.

Owned *me*.

Every inch of my body responded to his touch as he explored my curves with his skilled hands.

"This dress should be illegal." His words came out in a throaty whisper against my skin as he teased a trail of harsh kisses from my lips and along my neck. "Do you have any idea how fucking hard I've been all night long?" His carnal eyes locked with mine. "All because of how goddamn stunning you are." He cupped my cheeks, his fingers digging into my skin to the point it was borderline painful. "How goddamn *confusing* you are."

I parted my lips, about to ask what he meant by that. But before I could, he erased the little space between us, his mouth a breath away.

"But I don't care about any of that. Not now. Not when it's been so fucking long."

His lips fused with mine, and he walked me backward until my legs hit the desk. Moving his hands to my ass, he hoisted me onto the surface and forced my legs to straddle him. A moan slipped from my throat when he thrust against me, each movement pushing me higher and higher.

Making me desperate for more of this complex, intriguing, mysterious man.

"Gideon," I whimpered as he dragged his hand up the inside of my leg.

When he reached the apex of my thighs, he darted

his fiery eyes to mine, our labored breathing the only sound in the room.

"Imogene…"

"Yes," I exhaled.

"Are you telling me that, all night long, as I've watched you in a way that bordered on obsession, there's been nothing underneath this dress?" He ghosted his thumb against my center.

I cried out, but his touch was gone in a heartbeat. I attempted to squeeze my legs together, find some sort of relief from the throbbing ache, but he wouldn't let me.

"Tell me, Imogene." He cupped the back of my head.

"Yes."

I'd tell him anything right now if it meant he'd touch me.

"Is there a reason you're not wearing any panties?" He brought his lips to the column of my throat and peppered rough kisses along the skin. I wouldn't be surprised if I woke up tomorrow to find my flesh red and riddled with bite marks.

"Lines," I managed to say. "I didn't want any panty lines."

"And I hoped you were going to say it was so there'd be no barrier when I did this."

Before I could utter a response, he dropped to his knees and yanked me to the edge of the desk. Hiking up the skirt of my dress, he dragged his tongue up my center.

Relief flooded my veins, but it only lasted a moment before a renewed craving built inside of me, growing stronger with every swipe of his tongue.

"So delicious," he murmured. "So fucking wet."

He looked up at me, his lips coated with my desire. "Say it's for me."

"It is," I exhaled, digging my fingers into his hair.

When my nails scraped against his scalp, he groaned, pushing my thighs even wider and easing a finger inside before adding another one. I braced a hand on the desk, needing to feel somewhat grounded when the tantric rhythm of his tongue lapping at my clit made me feel like I was flying, each thrust of his fingers causing euphoria to crackle over me, a bomb on the verge of detonating.

My breathing grew ragged, my vision going fuzzy, blinding me to the reality of what we were doing. Anyone could walk in on us at any minute and see Gideon's face buried between my legs.

Liam could walk in at any minute.

But that wasn't enough to make him stop.

"Harder," I panted.

He craned his head back and met my eyes with a single brow raised.

"My clit. Bite me harder."

"My girl likes a little pain with her pleasure. Doesn't she?"

With a fiery look in his eyes, he returned to me, his teeth nibbling harder against me as his fingers fucked me with an almost punishing intensity. A jolt of pleasure surged through me, making me cry out as I straddled the thin line between madness and sanity.

And I didn't give a fuck who heard me. I needed this. It had been far too long since I'd been with someone who gave me what I needed. What I craved.

Who seemed to know my body, how to make me hum, make me vibrate, make me sing.

"Come on, Imogene," Gideon growled. "Don't hold back. Let me feel you. Let me hear you. Let me taste you."

He gave my clit another hard nibble, and that was all it took to send me over the edge, my body convulsing around him, his name a wanton benediction on my tongue. But he still didn't stop. Instead, he kept fucking me with his mouth, drawing out every ounce of pleasure until I had absolutely nothing left.

But he wasn't done with me. Anything but.

Shooting to his feet, he crushed his lips to mine, and I moaned at the taste of me on his lips.

"Do you see how incredible you taste?"

"Yes," I whimpered.

"Your cunt is a goddamn drug, Imogene. I need to feel you. Need to be inside you."

I reached for his waist and palmed his crotch, massaging his hard length. "Then what are you waiting for?"

"Goddamn," he groaned, making quick work of his belt and unzipping his pants. Then he focused his heated stare on me. "Take me out," he commanded.

Not breaking eye contact, I followed his demand, pulling him free and stroking him. Although he didn't need the help. He was so damn hard.

He pulled his wallet from the inside pocket of his suit jacket and retrieved a condom packet, ripping it open. But instead of rolling it on himself, he handed it to me.

"Put it on."

He may have been giving me an order, but it felt like he was giving me control. Giving me permission to step on the gas or slam on the brakes at any time.

But I didn't want to slam on the brakes. Not now. Not when I finally felt something.

Taking the condom from him, I ran my thumb along his tip, spreading the pre-cum around before rolling it on, just like Samuel taught me all those years ago.

"Good." He licked his lips. "Now bring me closer."

My pulse picked up even more as I followed his

request, an ache unlike any I'd ever experienced settling inside me, clawing at my bones.

"Let me feel you, Imogene." His voice was a raspy growl dripping with desperation.

He adjusted his stance as I guided him toward me, both of us moaning simultaneously when I brought him to my entrance. He closed his eyes, barely contained lust squeezing his face as he took several breaths.

When he returned his gaze to mine, it was filled with nothing short of raw hunger.

Removing my hand from his hard length, I hooked a single leg around his waist and pulled him closer.

"Fuck me, Gideon."

CHAPTER SIXTEEN

Imogene

Like a wild, untamed beast on the brink of losing all control, Gideon drove inside of me with a punishing force. I cried out, pain spiraling through me from the sudden invasion.

But that didn't make him stop. And I didn't want him to.

With every delicious thrust, I clutched him tighter, encouraging him to fuck me harder. Faster. Deeper, if that was even possible. He invaded my body so fully and completely that I doubted there would be anywhere inside me he hadn't claimed as his when we were finished.

"God, this cunt," he growled, picking up his pace, his body moving with a feral energy. "It was made for me."

He crushed his mouth to mine, his teeth digging into the sensitive flesh of my lower lip. "Made for me to fuck. To use. To control."

"Yes." His depraved words caused that dull ache deep in my core to become more pronounced yet again.

"Tell me, Imogene." His muscles clenched, and he brought a single hand up to my throat.

"It's yours, Gideon. Only yours."

He roared, his drives becoming even more punishing, his hold on my throat tightening slightly.

"Harder," I begged, and he picked up his pace. But that wasn't what I was talking about. "Your hand," I told him without a hint of trepidation. "Choke me harder."

A moment of uncertainty flickered in his expression as he slowed his motions to a stop and stared at me. I expected him to look at me like there was something wrong with me, much like Liam did the one and only time I asked this of him.

But Gideon didn't. Instead, he nodded, using the hand around my throat to guide me onto my back so I was flush against the surface of the desk.

"I might push your limits, Imogene. But I'm not going to hurt you. Won't give you more than I know you can handle. You can rest assured that you're safe with me. Do you understand?"

"Yes."

He bore his gaze into mine. "Do you trust me?"

I barely knew this man, but he'd already proven he didn't want to hurt me. Instead, I'd witnessed him take a life in order to save mine. That had to count for something.

"I do."

"If it becomes too much, tap my forearm three times."

His instructions rendered me momentarily speechless, a memory forcing its way to the surface.

Samuel had asked me to do the same thing.

Like Gideon, he never looked at me like there was something wrong with me when I'd shared my fantasies with him.

For the longest time, I'd kept them to myself for fear of what people might think, especially considering my father was one of the most prolific and sadistic serial rapists and killers. The last thing I should have wanted was to have someone choke me. To be interested in something like this after the way he'd treated women.

But Samuel didn't see any of that when he looked at me. Instead, he encouraged me to explore this side of myself, constantly assuring me there was nothing wrong with having certain cravings, especially if they were explored in a safe environment.

That was what Samuel gave me. A safe place.

He was my safe place.

"Imogene?" Gideon's voice snapped me back to the

present, and I stared deep into his blue eyes, everything about them so similar to Samuel's. Was that why I was doing this? Because some part of me wanted Gideon to be Samuel?

Or maybe I was here because I was finally ready to take back control of my life. To do something for myself.

Just like Melanie encouraged me to do earlier.

"Yes." I tapped his forearm three times, demonstrating that I understood what to do.

"Good girl." His stare became carnal and predatory as he thrust into me, going even deeper than before. I cried out but was quickly silenced when he tightened his grip around my throat, rendering me helpless and at his mercy.

And I loved everything about it. The panic. The uncertainty. The lack of control.

"You're such a good fucking girl," Gideon grunted as he continued his punishing rhythm. "Such a good fucking whore."

When I moaned, a smirk pulled on his lips. "You like that? Like me calling you a whore? Like the idea of me using this cunt?"

It sounded so depraved. So wrong. I shouldn't have wanted these things.

"It's okay." Gideon moved both hands to my cheeks and tenderly cupped them. "It's nothing to be ashamed of. Don't let your desires limit you, even if you consider it taboo or wrong. Let it empower you."

It had been so long since I'd been with someone who understood it. Who didn't question it. Who *wanted* to empower me.

Who didn't force me into the mold of who they wanted me to be.

"Yes."

"Yes?" Gideon arched a brow.

"Yes." I grabbed the back of his head, bringing his mouth to mine. I bit his lower lip. "I like hearing you call me your whore. Want you to use my cunt for your pleasure."

I felt him harden even more inside of me. Then a roar ripped from him as he returned his hands to my throat, fucking me harder still. I gasped for air, his grip on me cutting off most of my oxygen.

"That's right. Take my cock like the good little whore you are. You like it like this, don't you? Like being fucked hard."

My mouth grew wide, what little air I was able to suck in not enough. My body was wound tight, my vision going blurry as Gideon simultaneously deprived me of what I needed and gave me what I wanted.

"This cunt was made for me. You hear that, Imogene?" He curved toward me, his eyes barely an inch from mine. "This. Cunt. Is. Mine." His grasp on my throat tightened, leaving me completely at his mercy.

I struggled to breathe, my body's innate reaction to being choked. But I still didn't tap his arm, his punishing thrusts catapulting me over the edge. The first wave hit me like a tornado, unrelenting spirals of euphoria causing my body to shatter around him.

Gideon instantly released his grip, and I drew in my first lungful of air, which only caused my orgasm to intensify even more.

"Fuck, baby." He slammed his mouth against mine, breathing into me, giving me every last ounce of oxygen he possessed as he covered my heart with his hand.

I was so blissed out from the soul-crushing orgasm pummeling through me that I didn't even pause to think how Samuel used to do this precise thing after he'd deprived me of air. Like he physically needed the reassurance I was still breathing. That my heart was still beating.

Just like Gideon seemed to need.

Tearing his mouth from mine, he hauled me off the desk and onto my trembling legs. He spun me around and bent me over the surface. Wrapping his hand in my hair, he yanked my head to the side so I had no choice but to look into the ornate mirror covering one of the papered walls.

"Watch me fuck you, Imogene." He hiked my dress

back up to my waist and rammed inside of me from behind.

"Do you see how good you take me? How greedy your pussy is for me?"

"Yes," I moaned, unsure how much more of this I could take, each thrust bordering on painful, but in the best way possible.

From this angle, he felt even thicker. Even deeper.

Even more like Samuel.

I closed my eyes, pushing down the thought, but a harsh smack to my ass forced them open once more.

Gideon's breath heated my neck as he clamped his teeth onto my earlobe and tugged.

"I told you to watch me fuck you. Close your eyes again, and it won't be your ass I spank, but something much more sensitive." He brought his thumb and forefinger to my clit and pinched hard.

I cried, then moaned, moving against him, desperate to feel him thrust deep and hard once more.

He growled as he increased his pace, still pinching my clit, sensing I enjoyed the pain of it.

"That's what you get for being such a little tease, Imogene. For driving me fucking crazy tonight with this dress. It's been torture." He drove harder, his words strangled through his labored breathing. "Say it. Say this is what you deserve for being such a little tease."

I stared at our reflection in the mirror. "This is what I deserve," I panted.

"For what?" he ground out.

"For being such a little tease."

"Fuck," Gideon hissed, his nostrils flaring as he increased his rhythm. He pressed a hand between my shoulder blades and pinned me to the surface, not letting up until a roar tore through the room.

He moved both hands to my hips and spasmed through his release at the same time as I spilled over the edge with him. In an effort to draw out my orgasm, he slowed his motions, his rhythm becoming more sensual and seductive.

Once he seemed to have his breathing under control, he straightened and pulled out of me. Before I could attempt to right myself, he wrapped a protective arm around my waist and helped me. Moving his hands to my cheeks, he cupped my face and pressed his lips to mine.

This kiss felt different than all our previous ones. It still held that fiery passion and hunger, but there was an added sweetness to it, a slowness that made it more sensual.

More...personal.

More like Samuel.

He used to do the same thing after a particularly intense sexual experience, a way to reconnect, bring me back to reality.

How was this possible? How could he feel so much like Samuel? The way he moved. The way he breathed. The way he tasted.

It was too much.

Too heartbreaking.

Too debilitating.

I quickly tore my lips from his and pushed him away, adjusting my dress.

He blinked, taken aback by my sudden shift in demeanor.

"Imogene, are you—"

"This should *not* have happened," I managed to say through the lump building in my throat.

I refused to cry in front of this man after having sex with him. I needed to hold it together.

But it was so damn hard when he stared at me with those eyes.

Samuel's eyes.

"Imogene..." He took a hesitant step toward me, but I backed away, holding up a trembling hand in front of me, needing a barrier between us.

"I got caught up in the heat of the moment. In my memories. I guess I wanted you to be..." I squeezed my eyes shut and shook my head.

What was I going to tell him? That I just let him fuck me because of some crazy, misplaced hope that he *was* my dead ex-boyfriend?

"Well, it doesn't matter. All that does is that this…" I gestured between our bodies, "was a mistake. I can't…" I sucked in a quivering breath. "I just can't."

I spun on my heels and hurried out of the library, not wanting him to see me have a breakdown after having sex. And that was the problem.

It *wasn't* just sex. Not to me.

Being with Gideon made me *feel* again.

And that scared me more than anything.

"There you are."

At the sound of the familiar voice, I snapped my head up to see Liam strolling casually toward me. His easy gait and relaxed smile were a stark contrast to the tense energy consuming me.

A knot of unease tightened in my stomach as I tried to compose myself so he wouldn't pick up on the fact I'd just been fucked harder than I ever had before.

And in his library, no less.

That would have required Liam to be observant, though.

"I was wondering where you'd disappeared to."

"My feet were killing me so I went to sit down for a minute in the library. Guess I lost track of time. You know how I get around books."

A low chuckle rumbled from his throat as he kissed my forehead. "That I do." He lingered a beat longer than I felt comfortable with.

Could he smell Gideon on me? Did he see how flushed my skin was from the heightened state of arousal I was still in?

"Come on," he said when he finally pulled away. "I'd like one dance with the birthday girl now that your feet have had a rest."

"Of course."

Liam guided me down the hallway, his hand heavy against the small of my back. We only made it a few feet before the distinct sound of confident footsteps echoed behind us. I silently cursed under my breath when Liam paused, glancing over his shoulder.

"Mr. Saint." He turned to face Gideon. "I thought you'd left."

I reluctantly turned around, as well, my eyes drifting up to meet Gideon's of their own accord. The instant they locked on his intense gaze, an ache settled low in my belly.

"I'm heading out now. Thank you for your hospitality."

Liam offered his hand and they shook. "I hope you've enjoyed yourself."

I shifted nervously at the double meaning to his remark. Gideon seemed to find amusement in it, though, the corners of his mouth quirking up slightly.

"More than you can possibly imagine."

My cheeks heated as a renewed rush of electricity

coursed through me. I wished it didn't. Wished I didn't feel anything for this man. He brought out feelings in me I didn't think I'd ever experience again after losing Samuel.

I wasn't sure how to deal with that.

"Happy birthday, Ms. Prescott."

He held my gaze for a protracted moment, the seconds seeming to stretch as I stared into his blue eyes. Finally, he pushed past us and disappeared from view.

CHAPTER SEVENTEEN

Gideon

"Did anyone suspect you?" Henry asked the following morning after I updated him on everything that happened last night at Imogene's party.

Well, *almost* everything.

I left out what happened in the library. Not because I was ashamed. After all, he was fully aware I planned to use Imogene to destroy Liam, even if he'd repeatedly voiced his concerns about getting close to her.

And every time, I'd assured him I had the situation under control. That I didn't care about Imogene. That my priority still was, and always would be, making those responsible for what happened to Jonah and me pay.

Imogene was merely a pawn. Nothing more.

Although with every second I spent in her presence, I found myself becoming more drawn to her.

Case in point — last night.

I knew it was a bad idea the second I crushed my lips to hers. Hell, the second I walked into that room.

I'd reminded myself that using her like this was all part of my plan to eviscerate Liam's existence. It was why I was so rough with her. Why I choked her, called her a whore. I thought it would serve as a reminder of her purpose to me.

It wasn't supposed to make me feel anything for her.

But when I watched her nearly break into tears in front of me, I couldn't ignore the guilt gnawing at my stomach and eating at my soul.

I hated seeing her so broken.

Hated the knowledge that it was my fault — both Samuel *and* Gideon.

"I told you they wouldn't," I said confidently, taking a slow sip of coffee.

The sun streamed through the open French doors as I sat in the cozy breakfast nook, the entire space bathed in a warm, golden light. The soft breeze from the ocean wafted in, carrying the gentle roar of the waves crashing against the shore.

"After all, I'm a dead man." I winked. "None of them doubted my story for a second."

"None of them?" He arched a brow, a silent

reminder that there was one person who *could* put the pieces together, especially after last night.

I saw it in her eyes as she stared at me after I made her see stars. After I felt her body shudder.

After I kissed her with the same tenderness I once did.

I didn't know what had come over me. It was habit, muscle memory kicking in.

But when she pushed me away and looked at me with so much agony, I knew I had misstepped. Knew exactly what she was thinking about — our past.

Or, more accurately, her past with Samuel.

"Alton took the bait," I told Henry, ignoring his question. "Wants to discuss how he can make me even richer at the golf tournament next weekend. Which I've scored an invite to."

Henry choked on his coffee, coughing as he struggled to catch his breath. "Don't tell me you accepted."

"Sure did. Sent in my entrance fee this morning. It's for a good cause."

"Let me get this straight." He pinched the bridge of his nose, obviously irritated by this turn of events. "You just accepted an invite to the golf tournament Liam Pierce hosts every year to benefit the charity you once spearheaded. The golf tournament that's known as the Samuel Tate Invitational."

"And that's not all. I'll be playing on a foursome with Liam, Alton, and James. Just like old times."

"For fuck's sake." He clenched his fists, briefly squeezing his eyes shut. "You know I'll always have your back, right? That I completely support your reasons for wanting them dead?"

"It's why I trust you more than anyone else in my life."

"I don't like this, Sam."

I parted my lips to correct him, but he cut me off.

"Gideon. Sorry."

I nodded my acceptance of his apology. It was my first rule when we started down this path. I was no longer Samuel Tate. According to the world, he was dead.

And he would remain dead, no matter what happened.

"The more time you spend with these people, especially for any extended period of time, like at a golf tournament, the riskier it gets."

"I know the risks," I reminded him. "And I'm willing to take those risks to make these people suffer. If you think about it, everything's just become much easier."

"Easier?" Henry furrowed his brow. "Easier how?"

"Instead of trying to attack from outside the guarded walls, I've been invited in, just like we'd hoped."

"Don't forget what happened to you the last time you were on the inside."

I pinned him with a glare, my jaw ticking. "You honestly think I'll forget? Forget those bastards tried to kill me. Forget it was a miracle I survived in the first place, but only because some asshole wanted to make money off me. Trust me, Henry. I haven't forgotten. Not even when I spent years locked in a cell surrounded by the stench of death, only allowed out to train or fight. The reminder of what they did to me just to increase their wealth is etched in every single one of my scars. In this new face I wear because the old one had become too damaged."

With every word I spoke, my irritation increased, the horrors I'd faced on a daily basis flashing before my eyes. In those early days, I'd almost wished that bullet had killed me. It would have been better than the hell I'd been trapped in. But the more time I was locked up and subjected to the worst torture imaginable, the stronger my resolve grew.

The stronger my need for revenge grew.

It was what kept me alive.

So Henry needn't worry.

No matter what happened, I wouldn't forget my purpose.

He gave me a sympathetic smile. "I'm sorry."

"Don't apologize. You're just looking out for me, like you swore you would when we were stuck in that shitty foster home."

"That hasn't changed, nor will it ever. No matter what."

I held his gaze. "Thanks, brother."

Henry cleared his throat, not one to dwell on his feelings for longer than necessary. I wasn't either. "What do you need from me?"

The sound of my cell ringing cut through and I pulled it out of my pocket, looking at the number flashing on the screen.

"You can start by pretending to work for me." I handed him the phone.

"Any reason for that?"

"No doubt Alton did his research and creamed himself at the prospect of managing my investments."

"Very well." He grabbed my cell and stood from the table, stepping away from the open doors to answer the call.

I pulled myself to my feet and headed onto the terrace, the April sun heating my face as I took in the stunning view of endless ocean just a few yards away. I focused my attention on the rhythmic movements of the bodies bobbing up and down on the water.

A bubble of hope filled me at the idea of spotting Imogene amongst them.

But she wasn't there.

I briefly contemplated stopping by her place to make sure she was okay. That was the last thing I needed, though. I needed to stop worrying about her. Needed to remember my purpose, like Henry told me.

Not get distracted by a beautiful smile and sexy body. Remember she was merely a tool. Nothing more.

"You were right," Henry's voice cut through.

"About?" I spun around.

He strolled toward me and handed me my phone. "That was Sinclair's assistant. She indicated he hoped to set something up with you sooner rather than later. Even offered to stay in town a little longer to cater to your availability."

"What did you tell her?"

"I mentioned you had a rather full schedule this week, but you could carve out an hour of time this afternoon if he didn't mind coming to you. Looks like today's the day you set that trap."

"Which might not have been possible if I hadn't been at that party last night," I reminded him. "He wouldn't have been so quick to reach out."

"You're probably right," Henry admitted with a sigh. "Doesn't mean I can't be worried about you, considering I'm fully aware of what these assholes are capable of."

"True, but this won't be like last time. Now, do you think you can find someone to pretend to be a house-keeper or assistant in order to keep up the ruse that I'm a billionaire?"

"You *are* a billionaire," he reminded me. "But I'm

already one step ahead of you. I called Willow and told her I needed her today."

"I hope you pay her well with all the shit you put her through."

"Don't worry. She's well taken care of. And these days, it's more like all the shit *you* put her through."

"I knew I could count on you."

CHAPTER EIGHTEEN

Imogene

"Good morning, sunshine," I said brightly when Melanie finally emerged into the living room a little before noon, her dark hair disheveled.

"It's official." Her eyes were barely open as she shuffled toward the coffee machine and popped a pod into the one-cup brewer. Then she grabbed a glass and filled it with water from the refrigerator, practically downing all of it. "I can't drink like I used to."

I laughed as I took a sip from my own coffee. "Join the club."

She did a once-over of me. "You seem just fine."

"Because I stopped drinking when we left Liam's. I certainly didn't let anyone at the bar talk me into doing shots." I gave her a knowing look.

While I initially had no desire to go to a bar once we left Liam's stuffy party, Melanie talked me into it. Said she needed to reconnect with the common folk after being surrounded by high-strung businessmen and their stuck-up wives. So I indulged her, and we stopped by a bar a few blocks up the street for what I thought was just going to be one drink.

I was wrong.

At least it took my mind off what happened with Gideon, if for only a few hours.

"I used to be able to handle tequila, no problem." She held her stomach before adding a touch of milk and sweetener to her coffee. With sluggish steps, she made her way onto the couch and plopped down beside me, taking a much-needed sip of caffeine. "If I ever try to do shots again, remind me how I feel right now."

"You got it."

"So tell me..." She faced me, slowly coming back to life now that she'd had some coffee, her eyes sparkling with curiosity. "What were you doing last night when you disappeared from the party?"

"I don't—"

"Or perhaps the question I should ask is *who* you were doing."

As much as I wanted to leave what happened with Gideon in the past, I was desperate to talk to someone about it. Hell, I hoped to tell her last night, but based on her inebriated state, she wouldn't have remembered this morning.

"We had sex," I blurt out.

"Please tell me you're not talking about Liam, because you know how I feel about that fucked-up arrangement."

I waved her off. "No. Not Liam." I took a sip of coffee. "Gideon."

Her mouth dropped open, eyes widening.

It took a lot to make Melanie Burnham speechless. But my admission did precisely that.

"Seriously, Gin? I mean, I was hoping you'd admit you kissed, maybe got some finger-fuck action. But you had sex with Gideon Saint during your birthday party and didn't tell me until now?!" she shrieked.

"Why don't you broadcast it so all of Southern California knows?"

"You can't blame me for being relieved that you've finally slept with someone." She straightened, this information seeming to make her hangover disappear. "Tell me everything." Her eyes lit up as she leaned into me. "How was it? How did it happen? Where did it happen? Was he as amazing as I imagine he is? When are you seeing each other again?"

"Slow down, Mel. I..." I trailed off, trying to get my

thoughts in order. "I don't really know how it happened. One second, I was telling him about the scavenger hunt Samuel planned for me. The next, I was kissing him."

A surge of electricity coursed through my body, igniting every nerve ending as I recalled the warmth of his lips on mine. It wasn't just a kiss. It was a claiming, the way his mouth all but owned me.

"The next, we were doing a lot more than just kissing."

"How was it?"

I shook my head, trying to find the words to adequately explain how last night was. It had been so long since I'd experienced anything remotely close to the intensity and passion I did with Gideon.

"Perfect," I finally answered. "It was exactly what I needed. At least that's what I convinced myself in the heat of the moment. It was why I went as far as I did."

Her expression fell. "And when the moment fizzled out?"

"I did, too."

"What happened?"

I pinched my lips together and stared blankly ahead.

How could I explain it? How could I put into words why Gideon stirred up emotions and memories I'd been fighting to bury for years?

"He felt so much like Samuel," I choked out.

"Imogene...," Melanie sighed, resting her hand on my arm, warm and comforting. "You can't live your life thinking every man with blue eyes could be your long lost love. Samuel's dead. I wish he weren't. Wish he were still here. No doubt you two would be married and have an entire basketball team of little kids running around because of all the sex you'd be having. But he's gone." She squeezed my arm. "And he's not coming back."

"I know that. My *mind* knows that." I hesitated as I sipped on my coffee. Then I leaned toward her again. "He moved like him. Tasted like him. Held me like him. He *felt* like him when he was inside me. And then..."

"Yes?"

"Samuel used to do this...thing." I pulled on the hem of my shirt, shifting on the couch. "Whenever things got intense in the bedroom—"

"You mean when he fucked you so hard it made the walls shake?"

I gaped at her, my eyes bulging out of their sockets.

"I heard you two a few times I came home early from class." She shrugged, as if it weren't a big deal.

I should have been horrified she'd overheard us having sex, but it didn't seem to faze Melanie. Not much did.

"So Samuel used to do a thing after a particularly rough pounding?" she prodded me to continue.

"Right. Of course."

I squared my shoulders, pushing down my unease at the idea of talking about this with Melanie. But if I couldn't share this with her, who could I?

"He'd sort of...bring me back to earth, in a manner of speaking. Would pull me into his arms and kiss me. Gideon did the same exact thing last night."

"*What?*" she exclaimed, eyes widening once more. "He *kissed* you after fucking you?" She feigned disbelief. "That *is* strange. We should definitely launch a full investigation into this unusual occurrence. I mean, nobody kisses after sex. It's so absurd."

With every word she spoke, the sarcasm in her tone grew thicker and thicker.

"That's not what I mean," I protested. "It wasn't the fact he kissed me that freaked me out. It was *how* he kissed me. It was slow. Soft. Like he was reminding me who we were to each other. Bringing me back to reality, more or less."

"And because Gideon did the same thing, you... what? Think Samuel has come back from the grave?"

"He felt so much like him. So much so that I sort of freaked. Told him it was a mistake. That it can't happen again."

"Let me see if I have this straight." She set her mug on the coffee table and fully faced me. "You had sex with the man you haven't been able to stop thinking about since you met him a week ago, and you told him it was a mistake because you think his dick feels a little too much like your dead ex-boyfriend's?"

"When you put it like that, it sounds crazy."

"Because it *is* crazy, Gin." She took my hands in hers, squeezing them. "You enjoyed yourself last night, right?"

A shiver trickled down my spine from the memory of Gideon's body moving in time with mine. How he seemed to know exactly what to do to push me higher and higher until I unraveled around him.

"More than I have in a long time."

"Then don't run from this. I get things are complicated, that Samuel still owns a big piece of your heart. And that's okay for him to have a piece. But only a piece. It's been five years since he died. It's time to move on. To open yourself up to the possibility of finding someone to own the other pieces of your heart. And I think Gideon might be really good for you, if for no other reason than you've finally slept with someone other than Liam."

"I know. I just..."

"You can't help but feel like you're betraying Samuel," she finished before I could get the words out.

I closed my eyes and nodded, a lone tear trickling down my cheek. That was precisely what it all boiled down to. Maybe if they'd found his body, I wouldn't have held onto the idea of him still being alive like I did. I feared a tiny part of me would always hold on to that hope until proven otherwise.

"I saw how devastated you were when they found Samuel's car." She squeezed my hand. "When the police said there was no way anyone could survive losing that amount of blood. But you can't keep doing this to yourself. You need to live your life. Samuel would want you to be happy." She narrowed her gaze. "Does Gideon make you happy?"

I opened my mouth, trying to formulate a response. I wasn't sure how to answer that. I'd never really thought about it. I wasn't sure I knew Gideon well enough to say he made me happy.

"He makes me feel…"

"Yes?" Melanie prodded.

"That's it. He makes me feel."

"If you ask me, that's a step in the right direction."

"Except I ran out on him after telling him having sex was a mistake."

She shrugged, grabbing her coffee and slinking back against the couch. "Explain the situation to him."

"You want me to tell him I freaked because he reminds me too much of my dead ex?"

"You don't need to go into *that* much detail, at least not right away. But you can at least open up to him. Tell him your fears. If he's worth your time, he'll understand."

"And if he doesn't?"

"Then he was never worth it to begin with." She grabbed the remote and powered on my TV, scrolling through my movies and settling on one of our all-time favorites, *The Count of Monte Cristo*. "But I have a feeling this one will be worth it."

I brought my coffee back to my mouth. "That's what I'm scared of," I muttered under my breath.

CHAPTER NINETEEN

Gideon

All my attention was focused on the monitors surrounding me as I watched a woman in a charcoal pencil skirt stride into my foyer, her heels clicking against the marble floors.

"Mr. Sinclair, I presume?" Willow greeted with practiced poise as she answered the door.

Alton stepped into my house. "And you are?" He held out his hand for her.

"I'm Mr. Saint's assistant, Willow."

His eyes flamed with appreciation as he gave the leggy redhead a once over.

"If I didn't want these fuckers to pay for what they did to Jonah, I'd go out there and punch him right now for the way he's looking at her," Henry seethed.

I glanced at him, his jaw clenched, eyes glued to Alton's every move. "Willow can handle herself, even if he *is* a creep."

"I know. I just…"

"What?" I pushed.

"I don't like the idea of him looking at her like that. That's all."

"Any reason for that?"

"She's my assistant," he replied dismissively.

"Is that *all* she is?"

"What are you insinuating?" He darted his gaze toward me.

"Just that you seem to be quite protective of her." I gave him a knowing look.

He could deny it all he wanted to, but I'd seen the way he looked at Willow.

"Like I said, she's my assistant. Not to mention, I'm forty-two. She's twenty-four."

"But you *have* thought about it."

I smirked, knowing all too well what his answer was. "And to think you gave me shit when I first got together with Imogene all those years ago because I was thirty and she'd just turned twenty-one. How old was Willow when you were thirty? In first grade?" I teased. I was the last person to care about an age difference. I knew better than anyone that age was just a number.

"Fuck off and focus, you asshole."

I returned my attention on the monitors, watching Willow escort Alton through the bright living area with floor-to-ceiling ocean-front views, and down a long corridor, following their path on various screens until they reached my office at the end of the east wing.

"Please have a seat." Willow gestured to the chair I'd instructed her to offer him. "Mr. Saint is finishing up on another call, but he should be with you in a few moments. Can I get you anything while you wait? Coffee? Tea? Perhaps something a little stronger?"

"How about you?" he crooned, his southern drawl pronounced. "Are *you* on that menu?" He ran a finger along her arm.

"Easy," I warned Henry, tension radiating from him. His nostrils flared, his jaw wound so tight I was confident it was about to pop. "He can't know you're involved."

"I know."

"Good."

I returned my attention to the screen as Willow pretended to blush at Alton's inappropriate remarks before politely excusing herself and retreating from the room. His gaze remained fixated on her every step of the way until she disappeared behind the door.

"Goddamn," he groaned, facing forward and discreetly adjusting himself.

Which only pissed off Henry even more, but he controlled himself.

He may not have had to suffer the years of torment I did, but he still wanted justice after what those fuckers did to Jonah.

A few seconds later, the door opened and Willow slipped into the tiny room. The sweet expression she wore in the office was now replaced with a fierce scowl.

"Did you hear that shit?" She crossed her arms in front of her chest.

"Told you he's a scumbag," I replied.

"He's lucky I didn't snap one of those pudgy fingers when he touched me."

I stole a glance at Henry, who looked ready to break not just every bone in his hand, but in his entire body.

"In a few days, he's going to wish the worst of his troubles was a few broken fingers," I assured her.

"Good." Willow's voice was laced with venom.

"You left the papers where he'd see them?"

She gestured toward one of the monitors. I followed her line of sight as Alton leaned over my desk, seemingly focused on one paper in particular.

"Bingo," Henry remarked when Alton whipped out his phone and began snapping photos of the document.

"That's my cue." I rose from my seat, straightening my crisp suit jacket before heading toward the door.

"Good luck," Willow offered.

"Thanks."

I stepped into the hallway and closed the heavy

wooden door behind me. I had no doubt Alton was already itching to get back to his office with what he uncovered in the papers I'd purposefully left out for him to find.

Little did he know his lack of ethics was about to cost him everything.

And I couldn't wait.

"Ah, Mr. Sinclair," I greeted jovially as I entered my office.

Alton whirled around, his eyes widening briefly like a kid who was caught with his hand in the cookie jar.

Instead, he was an investment banker caught documenting inside information that he planned to use to his advantage in order to make himself richer.

"Call me Alton," he instructed as he returned his phone to his pant pocket.

"Sorry to keep you waiting, Alton. Some of the other investors in my venture capital group had some concerns we needed to address." I approached him and shook his hand.

"Of course. You seem to have your eggs in many baskets, based on some research I've done."

"What can I say?" I skirted around my desk and lowered myself into the chair. "I'm a sucker for an innovative idea. I've backed a few misses, but I'm happy to say they've been mostly hits."

"No need to explain to me. I understand it all

perfectly. Sometimes you have to take a few risks to reap huge rewards."

"Exactly." I leaned back into my chair and tented my fingers in front of me. Then I widened my gaze, pretending to have just noticed the open folder on the desk.

"My apologies." I gathered the pages and quickly hid them in the file. "I'd asked my assistant to file these before bringing you in." I rolled my eyes, feigning annoyance. "Apparently, she didn't understand the instructions."

"Good help is hard to find these days," Alton said.

"Yes, it is. But at least she's nice to look at." I waggled my brows, playing the part of a chauvinist asshole, much like Alton.

"She's better than nice. I'm not sure how you get any work done with a little thing like that around."

"It does take quite a bit of resolve."

"Well, you're a better man than me. And you don't have to worry about any papers you left out. Any information you share with me directly or indirectly will always be kept in strict confidence, regardless of whether we have a professional relationship." A calculating grin curved on his mouth.

"But I do hope you'll consider moving some of your investments to my firm. I pride myself on individualized attention that you won't get at some of the larger firms.

You won't be handed off to some junior portfolio manager, either. If you agree to work with me, you'll only work with me."

"Okay then. You've piqued my interest. How do you plan on making me even richer than I already am?"

CHAPTER TWENTY

Imogene

I gazed out the window as my chauffeured car wound along the famous 17 Mile Drive in Pebble Beach. The landscape was a vibrant display of perfectly manicured greens, each one framing a picturesque view of the ocean.

It was a bit ironic to think that the annual fundraising event for Samuel's charity was a golf tournament in Pebble Beach. He despised golf. Worse, he hated the type of people who were able to afford to golf at Pebble Beach.

But when I started researching ways to keep Samuel's charity going after his death, Liam essentially took over, claiming something like this could bring in a fortune.

He wasn't wrong.

For the past few years, this one event alone had generated enough money to keep the charity running for an entire year. It also allowed it to expand its reach, providing more at-risk kids with a place to learn valuable skills in the hopes of avoiding a life of crime.

Despite all the good that came from the funds raised, a part of me couldn't help but feel like this was just another way for Liam to put on a show and impress everyone.

As the car drew near the entrance of the hotel, a swarm of eager photographers lined the road, their cameras poised and ready to capture shots of the numerous celebrities Liam's annual tournament attracted.

After a brief stop at the security gate, where the guard checked my name against the guest list, the Town Car crawled toward the front entrance. Within seconds of stopping, a valet attendant approached to open my door.

"Do you need help with your luggage, ma'am?" he asked as I stepped into the sunlight. The temperatures were lower up here than in San Diego, but it was still comfortable.

"That's not necessary." I shrugged my oversized purse onto my shoulder, then reached for the handle of my small roll-aboard suitcase. "I travel light."

"Of course, ma'am. Check-in is just inside and to your right."

I offered him my thanks, then followed his directions into the ornate lobby. The elegant space was a blend of dark wood and light walls, giving off an air of sophistication and luxury. Several people lounged on oversized couches, their conversations filling the room. The men were most likely discussing the stock market while the women were dishing on the latest gossip within their social circles.

It was the same conversations I'd heard countless times at similar gatherings.

"You're finally here!" A pair of arms assaulted me, nearly knocking me over.

"I'm finally here," I repeated, returning Melanie's hug.

"It's about damn time."

Not giving me a chance to check-in, she hooked her arm through mine, leading me through the lobby and toward the open French doors.

We stepped onto the rear terrace, more pristine greens stretching out before us leading to the crystal blue ocean just beyond it.

"If I had to suffer through any more conversations about how difficult it is to find reliable help so these uptight bitches don't have to change a diaper, I was going to lose my ever-loving mind."

She didn't even attempt to keep her voice low. It wasn't like it was a secret, though. Melanie would say the same thing to your face that she said behind your back and not think twice about it.

I'd never been like that.

In a way, I shared a lot in common with Liam, always worried how people viewed me. While Liam was desperate to prove to his grandparents that they were wrong about him, I was desperate to prove to the world I was nothing like my sperm donor.

That even though his DNA ran through me, I was my own person.

It wasn't until I met Samuel that I learned to let go of those fears. He made me see it didn't matter what people thought about me. The only thing that mattered was how *I* viewed myself. He taught me to embrace my true self, even the parts society may deem as dark or taboo. Told me not to be ashamed by some of my hidden desires. They didn't make me a bad person. Instead, he showed me how to be empowered by them.

Much like Gideon did the other night.

"Imogene," a familiar voice laced with warmth and love soothed as I approached an arrangement of wicker couches and chairs, leaving my suitcase off to the side. A handful of people sat around a coffee table, holding a glass filled with either a Bloody Mary or mimosa.

"Hey, Mama." I walked into her open arms and basked in her embrace.

I was lucky to have a great relationship with my mom. For so much of my life, we were all each other had, especially in those early days when we were living with a complete sociopath.

While I didn't regret my decision to leave Atlanta, I did miss having her close by.

"I'm so glad you're okay." She pulled back, concern etched in the lines of her face. Her auburn-tinted blonde hair fell down to her shoulders in waves, her cheeks slightly red from the sun. "Why didn't you tell me about those necklaces? You can't keep these things from me, Imogene. It's only going to make me worry about you even more, especially being so far away."

"I honestly thought it was just some fanatic," I replied dismissively, giving her the same response I had each time I'd spoken to her since that night.

"But still. You—"

"She's fine, Julia," a voice with an Australian accent interjected.

I stepped away from my mom and beamed at the man approaching, his blue eyes shining with all the affection of a father. He enveloped me in his embrace, leaving a soft kiss on my head.

"How you going, kid?" Lachlan asked.

"I'm *going* just fine," I replied, playfully mocking his use of the Australian phrase.

"Been out on your board?" He nodded toward the ocean glimmering in the distance.

"Every chance I get."

Although, I hadn't been surfing this past week, even after my doctor cleared me. Since my birthday party, I'd intentionally avoided going anywhere I might run into Gideon. Which meant avoiding surfing and taking Ollie to the beach.

"That's my girl." Lachlan gave me one last hug, filling me with a sense of comfort and love.

His DNA may not run through me, but since he met my mom over fifteen years ago, he's filled the role of my father and then some. He taught me how to surf. Came to as many of my soccer games as he could, even when he was playing professional baseball. He even taught me how to drive. In my eyes, Lachlan Hale was my father.

"You're sure you're okay?" Mama pressed. "The police still haven't found the guy who sent those necklaces, have they?"

"Not yet," I admitted.

Truthfully, it was somewhat unsettling he hadn't been found, but I wasn't going to let that interfere with my life.

"Even so, there haven't been any more...incidents

since that night. I'm fine." I squeezed her hand. "I'm safe. Don't worry."

"I'm your mother. I'm *always* going to worry about you." She pushed out a long breath. "But I get it. You need to live your life."

"Exactly."

I turned my attention to the rest of the people sitting in the lounge chairs.

"Mr. Burnham," I greeted as Melanie's father stood and wrapped me in a hug, kissing my cheek.

Despite being in his sixties, he was in incredible shape, his years as a Navy SEAL, then owner of the premier private military firm in the country evident in his physique.

"I told you, Imogene. Call me Alexander."

"I know." I laughed slightly. "Southern etiquette is hard to break."

"She's right about that," the tall brunette at his side said sweetly. "I'd spent a lot of my childhood in Charleston. You grow up learning to address all adults as Mr., Mrs., Miss, sir, or ma'am."

"Exactly." I sent Melanie's mother, Olivia, a smile before turning my attention back to her father. "But I'll work on it...Alexander."

"Good." He winked.

"And how are you doing, dear?" Olivia gave me a

tight hug before holding me at arm's length. "Are you enjoying life in San Diego?"

"Definitely." I beamed as Melanie approached with a fresh mimosa and handed it to me. "Especially now that I'm within driving distance of Mel instead of a five-hour flight."

"Liam, too," Olivia said. "It's like the old gang is finally back together again." Her expression fell. "Well…almost."

"Yeah." I swallowed hard, a twinge of sadness squeezing my chest at the reminder of Samuel, but I quickly pushed it down, brightening my voice. "Speaking of Liam… Is he around here somewhere? I told him I'd find him when I got here."

"Don't worry about him," Melanie admonished. "He's a big boy and can take care of himself." She moved closer, dropping her voice. "Just worry about yourself. Doing things that make *you* happy." She pinned me with a stare, tilting her champagne flute toward mine.

"I'll try my best."

"Good."

We clinked glasses and I brought my drink to my lips, the champagne with a splash of orange juice instantly relaxing me.

Until that same sensation of being watched trickled down my spine, all the tiny hairs on my body standing on end.

I discreetly looked around the terrace, inhaling a sharp breath when my eyes locked on Gideon's heated stare, his sparkling blue depths seeming to only see me.

I was instantly transported to last weekend. Him finding me in the library. His body tempting me as he drew near. Succumbing to this attraction as he gave me more pleasure than I'd experienced in years.

Maybe ever.

"Speaking of doing things that make you happy," Melanie murmured.

"What's he doing here?" I hissed softly.

I'd expected to spend the weekend with my friends and family. Seeing Gideon Saint hadn't factored into that at all.

"My guess is Liam invited him since he's loaded. But I think you should go ask. Make sure he's not crashing the party." With a sarcastic grin, she gave me a not-so-gentle push toward Gideon.

My nerves spiked at the thought of talking to him after the way I ran out on him the last time I saw him.

But what was I going to do? Avoid him all weekend?

Maybe his presence here was the sign I needed to just get over my fears and finally take a risk.

To stop clinging to a ghost.

To finally live my life again.

CHAPTER TWENTY-ONE

Gideon

I kept my eyes trained on Imogene as she moved across the terrace toward me, her sundress flowing with her measured motions. With every step she took, my pulse increased slightly.

I hadn't been this close to her since she ran away from me at her birthday party.

I couldn't say I hadn't seen her, though.

All week, I'd kept a close watch on her, but did so from afar. I didn't want to spook her even more by making her think I was some creepy stalker.

I *was* some creepy stalker, but I didn't want her to know that.

"Imogene," I greeted as she approached. A gentle

breeze lifted her hair and carried her sweet scent toward me. "You look well."

"Thanks." Her cheeks turned red under my compliment, and she averted her gaze, smoothing a strand of hair behind her ear.

I knew this look. She was nervous. It was obvious she didn't approach me just to be polite. There was another reason.

She closed her eyes, pinching her lips together into a tight line, as if giving herself a mental pep talk. Finally, her gaze drifted up to mine.

"About last weekend..." She shifted on her feet.

"Don't worry about it." I held up a hand. "You're right. It probably *was* a mistake. We can just forget it ever happened."

Although I doubted I'd ever forget just how damn incredible she tasted. How amazing she felt as she unraveled under my touch, her body just as responsive as it was all those years ago.

"What if I don't want to forget?"

My eyes widened slightly as I raked them over her. I'd assumed she approached me to clear the air, make sure this weekend wasn't too awkward, considering we were bound to cross paths on multiple occasions. It was such an Imogene thing to do, always the peacemaker.

"You don't?"

She slowly shook her head. "I don't. Not anymore,

anyway. Not now that I've had time to think. There are things you should know. I guess I—"

"Ah, you're finally here," a booming voice interjected.

The unexpected interruption caused Imogene to jump, instinctively increasing the distance between us. Liam swooped her into his arms and pressed a kiss to her cheek, completely ignoring me.

I had a feeling it was intentional.

"You missed all the fun last night."

"I told you. I couldn't miss the game. But I'm here now."

"Yes, you are." He grabbed her hand and started to lead her away. "Come on. Let's go see your parents."

She hesitated, her feet remaining rooted to the spot. It was only when she didn't automatically follow his command like the obedient little dog he wanted her to be that he glanced my way.

"Ah, Mr. Saint." He extended his hand toward me. "I didn't see you there."

I fought to bite back what I really wanted to say. He absolutely *did* see me. He just needed to feel in control, especially when it came to Imogene. With me in the picture, he was losing more and more of that control.

Hell, with me in the picture, he would soon lose everything.

It was exactly what I'd planned. But with every day, I

felt more and more remorse over the idea of using Imogene to fulfill that goal.

"Why would you, with a woman as beautiful as Imogene standing here?"

"You're right about that." He wrapped a possessive arm around her waist, holding her tightly against him. "If you'll excuse us..."

"You're welcome to join us, too," Imogene offered, managing to free herself from Liam's hold. "I'm sure my parents would love to meet you after everything you've done for me. Unless you have other plans, of course," she added quickly.

A slow smile curved my lips when I saw the irritated look on Liam's face, his mouth pressed together, his features tightening.

"I'm always willing to rearrange my schedule for you, Ms. Prescott."

Her gaze drifted to mine as she bit her lower lip, a blush blooming on her cheeks. Then she turned and strolled across the terrace, her hips swaying with her steps. As I followed, I felt Liam's annoyance with me increase, but he'd never openly show it in front of all of these wealthy people.

"Mama, Lachlan, I'd like to introduce you to Gideon Saint," Imogene said as she approached several wicker chairs and couches arranged around a coffee table. "Gideon, these are my parents, Julia and Lachlan Hale.

Gideon helped me a few weekends ago," she explained without going into too much detail.

I squared my shoulders, remembering the part I needed to play. "Pleasure to meet you both." I extended my hand toward her mother.

But instead of shaking it, she pulled me into her arms. "Thank you so much," she said softly.

I briefly closed my eyes, a tiny ball of guilt settling in the pit of my stomach.

Not only was I deceiving Imogene and Melanie with my lies, I could now add their parents into the mix.

Julia had been nothing but kind and supportive of Imogene and me when we were together. She didn't even blink at the nine-year age gap between us, even back then. If anything, she understood that love couldn't be constrained by age, considering she'd fallen for a much younger man herself.

"I simply did what needed to be done."

I could feel Liam's ire from several feet away. He'd always hated whenever someone else was the center of attention. This must have been killing him. He'd be the center of attention soon enough. Just not in the way he hoped.

"Regardless, I'm forever in your debt." She glanced at the tall, built man at her side. "We both are."

I shook Lachlan's hand, who also gave me his thanks,

neither one of them any the wiser I wasn't who I said I was.

"And these are *my* parents," Melanie offered, and I turned my attention to the man and woman sitting across from her. "Olivia and Alexander Burnham."

"Pleasure." I shook Olivia's hand, then shifted my gaze toward Alexander.

He was probably the most intimidating man I'd ever met. That was saying something, considering I'd spent four years fighting in death matches at least once a month.

Yet none of those men scared me like Alexander Burnham. With his sharp attention to detail, he exuded an aura of strength and control that made even the toughest men quiver.

He was one of the reasons Henry didn't think it wise for me to come this weekend. It was one thing to immerse myself in Imogene's life. To pretend to be someone else around Liam, Alton, and James in the hopes of making them pay.

It was another thing to spend the weekend in close proximity to Alexander Burnham.

The man was a Navy SEAL. He may have left the SEALs years ago in order to take over his father's private military firm, but he was still an intimidating man. To say he was observant would be an understatement.

I'd convinced Henry and myself it would be okay. If

I could successfully deceive Imogene, a woman I once shared a bed with, surely I could fool Alexander Burnham.

But as he raked his analytical stare over me, I worried I'd overplayed my hand. That my desperation for revenge caused me to be careless, like Henry warned. I couldn't let that show, though. This was a man who was trained to figure out when people were lying.

"Sir." I made sure to keep my eye contact even, not so much as licking my lips or shifting my weight between my feet as I waited for him to shake my hand.

"Gideon," he said finally, placing his hand in mine.

"Why don't you come have a seat?" Melanie hooked her arm through mine and dragged me toward one of the couches, gesturing to an open space.

Right next to Imogene.

I wanted to kiss her, especially when she sat on the other side of Imogene, ensuring that Liam couldn't sit next to her.

Hell, he couldn't sit anywhere, all the spots taken.

"So, Gideon, do you golf?" Julia asked.

"I do," I began.

"But..." she prodded, sensing there was more.

"But I hate it," I admitted, causing a ripple of laughter from everyone except Liam. Even Alexander managed to crack a smile.

The benefit of knowing these men in my past life

was that I knew all too well how they felt about golf. We'd often commiserated about the sport together.

Not Liam, though.

To him, being a member at several of the most prestigious golf clubs in the country was a status symbol. Something he aspired to.

Not something he avoided at all costs, like I did.

"Despite that, when I learned about the work this charity does, I happily paid the entrance fee."

"You could have just made a donation and not have to play golf," Liam interjected.

"And miss out on my opportunity to spend more time with all of you? I wouldn't miss it for the world, especially after the incredible time I had at Imogene's party last weekend."

I felt her stiffen beside me, especially when I casually draped my arm along the back of the couch.

Which also had me casually draping my arm along Imogene, too.

"It was one of the most memorable nights in recent memory."

Melanie choked on her drink, picking up on the double meaning to my statement. It was clear that Imogene told her what happened between us. I expected as much. Imogene didn't keep much from Melanie. Hell, Melanie was the only one who knew about us all those years ago, apart from Imogene's parents.

"And I have *you* to thank for the invitation." I smirked at Liam, watching as he fought to contain his mounting irritation with me.

"Like I said," he ground out, his smile growing faker by the second. "It was the least I could do after all you did for Imogene."

"I just did what any *decent* person would." I shifted my attention toward Imogene and gently took her hand in mine. When I noticed Liam's nostrils flare out of the corner of my eye, I went in for the kill. "And every day, I'm even more grateful I intervened."

She exhaled a tiny breath. "So am I."

"Oh, I completely forgot," Liam cut through, looking at his cell phone. "Imogene and I need to meet with the head chef to finalize tomorrow's menu."

Imogene straightened, pulling her hand from mine. "But you said—"

"It slipped my mind with everything else going on," he explained smoothly. "I promise it won't take too long. Once we're done, you can spend some more time with your parents since you haven't seen them in a while."

It didn't escape my notice he intentionally left me out of the equation. I expected nothing less from the little cockroach.

"All right," Imogene sighed, reluctantly pulling herself to stand. "I need to drop my bag off in my room first. I haven't even had a chance to check in."

"You can do that after. In the meantime, I'll have a bellman bring it up to mine, since your room is right next door."

Of course it was. He wouldn't have had it any other way.

"No need to go through the trouble," Melanie interjected. "I was about to head up to my room, so I'll bring it with me. When you're done, we can have some girl time."

"Sounds great."

"Why don't I join you?" Julia suggested as she stood. "I can at least offer some expertise when it comes to the desserts."

"That's not necessary," Liam began at the same time as Imogene said, "I'd love that."

"Great." She gave Imogene's arm a reassuring squeeze before looking my way. "It was great to meet you, Gideon. I'm sure I'll be seeing much more of you."

"I look forward to it." I shifted my eyes toward Imogene and held her gaze for a protracted beat before Liam dragged her away.

CHAPTER TWENTY-TWO

Imogene

Comfort surrounded me as I collapsed onto the plush, cloud-like bed in my hotel room, grateful for a moment to myself for the first time since I arrived here hours ago. While I was thrilled to have some much-needed time with my mama and stepdad, Liam had been wearing on me.

It was more than apparent he wanted to keep me away from Gideon, especially when I'd arrived at the event coordinator's office and learned Liam had already finalized the menu with the chef.

Years ago, Melanie had warned me something like this might happen if Liam and I slept together. Deep down, I knew she was right. But in the immediate aftermath of Samuel's death, I craved any kind of physical connection and didn't care about the potential conse-quences.

Now, I feared I'd pay the price for it.

Or, more accurately, my friendship with Liam would pay the price.

With a quick glance at the clock on the bedside table, I calculated whether I could afford to take a nap. If I didn't do anything overly extravagant with my hair for the welcome dinner tonight, I could probably rest for an hour.

After setting the alarm on my phone, I slipped under the fluffy duvet, not bothering to change out of my sundress. If I only had an hour, I didn't want to waste any time by searching for a pair of pajamas in my luggage.

Unfortunately, the instant I closed my eyes, a knock ripped through the space. I groaned, but reluctantly crawled out of bed and checked the peephole, assuming it was either Liam or Melanie.

To my surprise, it was neither.

Instead, Gideon stood in the hallway, looking just as delicious as he did earlier in his jeans and button-down shirt with the sleeves rolled up, revealing his toned forearms.

"Imogene," he greeted in a smooth, even tone when I opened the door.

"Gideon."

His gaze flickered down to the exposed cleavage of my sundress before returning to meet my eyes.

"I was hoping we could continue our conversation from earlier. I feel like we weren't quite finished yet. At least *I* wasn't."

A devious smile spread across his face, sending thousands of butterflies fluttering in my stomach. All it took was one look from Gideon Saint and I was putty in his hands.

"Of course." I pulled the door wide. "Won't you come in?"

"Thank you."

As he entered my room, his scent filled the space, bringing back memories of burying my face in the crook of his neck as he thrust inside of me. My heart raced at the thought of his hands on my body, his lips bruising mine.

This wasn't the first time I'd been alone with him. But it felt more intimate than any of our previous encounters, the atmosphere between us even more charged, considering I now knew how he kissed. How he tasted. How he moved.

How willing he was to push me to the edge of darkness, then pull me back to the light.

"Would you like something to drink?" I moved toward the wet bar and cracked open a bottle of whiskey, needing something to settle my nerves.

"No, thank you." He blew out a small laugh. "If I've learned anything over the past few weeks, it's that I need to keep my wits about me when I'm with you."

I poured some whiskey over ice and swallowed a large gulp before setting the glass onto the surface. "You do?"

With a deliberate nod, he stalked toward me with calculated strides, an animal hunting his prey.

Despite the way I ran from him the last time, I couldn't deny there was still a part of me that *wanted* him to hunt me. Wanted him to claim me as his.

Wanted him to own me.

"You mentioned you've had a change of heart." His voice was low. Deep. Husky.

"Y-yes." I squared my shoulders, fighting to hang on to what little control I had left. "I guess. I—"

"You guess?" he interjected. "I'd prefer something a bit more...firm, if you don't mind. Either you've had a change of heart or you haven't. If it's the latter, I'll leave and we can go back to denying ourselves what I can only classify as the most amazing sex I've ever had."

I inhaled sharply, his admission rendering me momentarily speechless. *I* thought it was pretty mind blowing, but I hadn't been having much sex these days. I figured Gideon had a long line of women hoping to sleep with him, especially with that mysterious billionaire vibe he gave off. And I was certain they were probably even more adventurous than me.

"It was the best sex you've ever had?"

"Without a fucking doubt, Imogene." He brought his hand up to my cheek.

I closed my eyes, basking in his warmth. It had only been a week since I'd last experienced his touch, but I physically ached for him.

"You brought out something I thought died years ago."

"You did, too. And that's what scared me. Not what we did." I laughed slightly, trying to ease the tension. "I liked what we did. Hell, I *loved* what we did."

"So you don't regret it?"

Keeping my eyes locked on his so he could see the truth within, I slowly shook my head. "Not anymore. Not now that I've had time to process everything." I draped an arm over his shoulder as I hoisted myself onto my toes, inching my mouth toward his. "In fact, I'd like to do it again."

He moved a hand to my hip, his hold resolute and commanding. Then he curved toward me, erasing the remaining space between us. But before he could kiss me, I pressed a finger to his lips.

"I just need you to promise me something first."

He straightened. "Whatever you need, Imogene. Say it, and it's yours."

"Just be patient with me. I haven't been with anyone in close to five years. Not like this anyway. Not when it means something to me."

"I mean something to you?" His normally determined voice faltered slightly.

His Adam's apple bobbed up and down as a flicker of something flashed in his eyes. I couldn't quite describe what it was. Guilt? Pity? Maybe surprise?

"You do. More than I thought possible after...well, after only knowing each other a short time," I explained, stopping myself short from bringing Samuel into this.

As much as I would always love Samuel, Melanie was right. It was time to let him go and move on. Find someone new who could make me happy.

I'd never be able to do that as long as I still clung onto his ghost as tightly as I had.

"I promise to be patient." Gideon brushed his warm lips against mine. "We'll take it at your pace, no matter how slow. After all..." He placed a hand on my hip, guiding me across the room and toward the bed. "Going slow can be just as pleasurable."

The slow, tantalizing rhythm of his body pulsing against mine set me on fire. Each movement was a seductive dance, each touch sparking a hunger I didn't think would ever be satisfied. At the feel of his erection circling against me, a whimper fell from my throat. Moisture pooled between my thighs, the blood in my veins growing hotter with every second I didn't feel his skin on mine.

"What do you think, Imogene?" he crooned in that provocative voice I'd heard in my sleep every night. That had me waking up with my hand between my legs. That had my vibrator seeing more use than it had all year.

"Think you can be satisfied going slow?"

I dragged my fingers through his hair, my nails digging into his scalp. He closed his eyes, relishing in my touch as I skimmed my lips against his.

"With you, I have a feeling I'll *always* leave satisfied."

CHAPTER TWENTY-THREE

Gideon

This was exactly what I wanted. Why I knocked on her door in the first place.

Despite Henry trying to persuade me that I didn't need Imogene anymore, I wasn't as convinced. Not with how obsessed Liam was with her. Hell, the sick fuck went so far as to pay a couple of assholes to kidnap her, for what purpose I still hadn't figured out.

I needed to do this. Needed Liam to watch as Imogene slipped away and not be able to do anything about it. Needed him to know how it felt to lose everything.

And Imogene *was* everything to him.

But now that I was with her, felt her lips on mine, I

couldn't help but feel guilty for the way I was using her. Hadn't she already been through enough?

Hadn't I already caused her enough pain?

Was that enough for me to walk away, though? I wasn't sure.

Worse, I was no longer sure if I was doing this as part of my plan for revenge, or because I was just as addicted to her today as I was all those years ago.

That was the problem with being an addict. It blinded you to any future complications. Nothing mattered except experiencing the high only that intoxicating elixir could provide.

Just like nothing mattered right now except experiencing the high Imogene's lips against mine always provided, her tongue tempting and torturing me, making me desperate for more of her.

Making me desperate for *all* of her.

"I need to see you," I panted as I tore my mouth from hers, trailing hot kisses along her jaw and burying my head into the crook of her neck.

I inhaled a deep breath of her intoxicating scent. There was a time I didn't think I'd ever smell it again. Thought I'd die surrounded by the stench of death and despair.

Now I wanted to drown in Imogene and never come up for air.

"You *do* see me," she teased.

"That's not what I'm talking about."

I ran a lithe finger down the column of her neck, along her collarbone, and between her breasts. When I teased her nipple, her breathing grew ragged, her eyelids fluttering closed.

"I need to see *all* of you. Need to taste your smooth skin. Need to run my tongue along every perfect inch of this body." I curved toward her, my lips a breath away from hers.

But instead of kissing her, I dipped my head toward her ear. "Need to watch your tits bounce while you ride me."

She released a tiny moan, the vein in her neck throbbing. I wanted to dart my tongue out and taste her skin, clamp my teeth on her as I marked her.

But I wanted this more. Wanted to drive her to the point of oblivion.

Abruptly dropping my hold on her, I stepped back and sat on the bed. "Let me see you, Imogene. Strip for me."

She blinked, my sudden shift momentarily surprising her.

Or perhaps frustrating her.

Then she reached behind her and pulled the halter tie securing her dress, allowing it to fall off her body. After she kicked it to the side, she stood in front of me in just a strapless bra and a pair of panties. The soft curves of her body glistened in the afternoon glow, beckoning to be touched and explored.

And I planned on doing just that.

"Your turn," she said breathlessly, her eyes filled with lust.

"Not yet."

"But—"

"You're still dressed, albeit barely. I asked to see all of you. So let me see you."

"Yes, sir," she replied coyly.

And damn if the devious smile that teased her lips didn't have my cock hardening even more.

She slowly unclasped her bra and was about to remove it when she turned away.

"Imogene," I growled.

"Yes?" she responded with feigned innocence, glancing over her shoulder as she dropped her bra onto the pile of clothes. She hooked her fingers into the sides of her panties. "Did you change your mind? Should I stop?"

"Don't you fucking dare," I seethed, my breathing growing labored.

"If you're sure."

"I'm sure, Imogene." I grabbed my throbbing erection through my jeans. "So damn sure."

"Very well then..." With a flirtatious gleam in her

eyes, she shimmied out of her lace panties, making a show out of bending over slightly as she did.

Finally, she turned around to face me, allowing me to see all of her. Everything about her was exactly as I remembered. Maybe even better. She was more mature now. Despite the familiarity of her body, there was one glaring difference, other than fuller breasts and hips.

The tattoo just below her hipbone, swirling patterns etched into her skin like a permanent love letter.

A promise.

A reminder of the unequivocal love she had for the man I once was.

But also a reminder that I'd been deceiving her these past few weeks.

That I'd continue to deceive her until she learned the truth.

"How's this, Mr. Saint?"

Her sultry voice pulled me out of my unease, sending a pulsing heat through me as she sauntered toward the bed and straddled me.

"Do you see enough of me now?"

She ground against me, and I could feel her heat through my jeans. But even that thin barrier was too much when all I wanted was to bury myself deep inside of her.

Keeping her body glued to mine, I lowered us onto the bed and flipped her so she was underneath me.

"Fucking beautiful." I lowered my lips to hers, my tongue tangling with hers in a soft kiss. My hand traveled the contours of her frame, imprinting each valley and curve to memory. It took everything inside of me not to trace the outline of her tattoo.

I wanted to. I'd drawn that exact symbol in that exact place so many times it was like second nature. Like an innate desire lived inside me, something in my brain sensing the need to trace that symbol on Imogene's hip whenever she was near.

But I couldn't. I'd made my decision. Chose my path.

It wasn't her.

At least I didn't think it was.

Now I was second guessing everything.

My mouth moved down her chest as my hand cupped her breast, my thumb and forefinger squeezing her nipple. Her whimper turned into a moan when I increased the pressure.

"You like that?"

"Yes."

"Think you'd like my teeth doing that, but harder?" I asked, even though I already knew the answer.

"Yes," she repeated.

"Good girl," I murmured, replacing my hand with my mouth.

My tongue teased her nipple, and she squirmed beneath me, desperate for me to do as I promised.

I bared my teeth, but only lightly scraped the sensitive bud.

"Gideon," she mewled. "Please."

"See how amazing it can be to go slow?" I traced another circle around her nipple before moving to the other one, smoothing my hand along her hipbone and toward the apex of her thighs. "How much more...satisfying it can be."

"I'm not so sure about that. Feels a lot more like torture to me."

"Ah, but that's where you're wrong." I scraped my teeth against her nipple as I inched my fingers closer to her heat. "A little pain makes your pleasure that much more enjoyable. Don't you agree?"

"Then let me feel the pain, Gideon."

"With pleasure."

Taking her nipple back into my mouth, I spread her slickness around her center. Then I pushed a finger inside at the same time as I bit her nipple. She clamped down on her lower lip, fighting back her screams as she pulsed against me, chasing her bliss.

"So fucking warm," I exhaled, stretching her to add another finger, hooking them around to hit the spot I knew drove her wild. "So fucking tight." I fought the urge to increase my motions, wanting her to feel every ounce of pleasure possible. "So fucking mine. You understand that, Imogene? If we're doing this, no one else gets to fuck this pussy."

"Yes," she exhaled, her breathing becoming more uneven.

But I still didn't go faster, adding another finger to stretch her out even more.

"Only I get to taste you. Only I get to touch you. Only I get to fuck you." I stole a glance at her. "That goes for any toys you may have, too."

She flung her eyes open. "You don't mean…"

Slowly nodding, I inched down her body, pushing her thighs wide. "I do. From this moment forward, I own every one of your orgasms. In return, I promise to make them the best damn orgasms of your life. Do we have a deal?"

I dragged my tongue along the seam of my lips, resisting the urge to dive in for a taste. It was fucking torture, being so close to her. *Smelling* her. Seeing her desire dripping down her thighs.

Finally, she nodded. "Only you get to taste, touch, and fuck me. No toys allowed."

"You can use toys," I corrected. "As long as I give you permission first. Now…" I pushed her thighs wider. "I want you to come all over my face."

Not wasting a second, I buried my face between her legs, the combination of my tongue on her clit and fingers inside of her causing her muscles to clench. Her motions increased, her moans intermingling with the sound of her slickness, and I knew she was close.

"Come on, Imogene," I encouraged. "Don't hold back. I want you to scream for me."

"I can't," she managed to protest through her labored breathing. "Not when—"

"Let him hear you. Then he'll finally know what you sound like when you don't have to fake an orgasm."

She didn't bother asking how I knew about Liam and her, too overcome with sensation. Her muscles tightened and I nibbled on her clit again. In a heartbeat, her body detonated around me, her pleasure soaring through her in waves.

And like I wanted, she didn't hold back, her cries of pleasure filling the room.

I didn't wait for her to come down. Didn't drag out her bliss. I needed to be inside of her. Needed to feel her pussy as it clenched around my cock.

Shooting to my feet, I unbuckled my belt and pulled my wallet out of my back pocket, fishing out a condom as she scrambled to her knees and reached for me. I was so clouded by lust and the need to be inside of her, I hadn't considered she'd try to remove my shirt until it was too late. The instant her fingers toyed with the top button, my hand flew up, wrapping around her wrist in a punishing grip.

"Don't," I growled, my voice harsh.

Her gaze flung wide as discomfort flashed in her expression.

I feared this would eventually come up. Feared she'd question why I'd insist on keeping my shirt on.

I didn't know if I could stomach letting her see why. Didn't know if I could handle the pity I would find on her face.

Or maybe the disgust.

I quickly loosened my grasp. "Sorry. I just... That's a hard limit for me."

She furrowed her brow. "What is? Letting me see you?"

"It is."

"Why?"

"Imogene..." My voice was a warning.

"Don't Imogene me," she snipped back. "Just tell me why."

"You really want to see why?" I growled, my voice coming harsher than I intended. I moved closer, causing her to back up until she hit the wall.

But she didn't waver in her determination, maintaining steady eye contact. "Please." She swallowed hard. "Don't shut me out."

Neither one of us said anything for several protracted moments, the only sound in the room that of our ragged breathing. Then I yanked at my shirt, causing the buttons to skitter across the floor, revealing myself to her.

"Happy now?" I seethed as she dipped her eyes to my torso, her sharp intake of air telling me everything I needed to know about what she thought.

Then she stepped closer, her gaze returning to mine as she hesitantly reached out to me. But she didn't touch me yet. As if waiting for permission.

Despite my better judgment, I gave a subtle nod of my head.

Her fingers brushed against one of the many scars that now marred my frame.

"What happened?" she asked in a pained voice.

"Car crash," I lied, not stopping her as she continued to explore my body, tracing the lines of several scars that were my inescapable reminder of the years I spent in captivity.

Of the hell I endured day after day.

It was why I kept them. Why I refused to go through any treatment that would dull their appearance. Not just because I wanted Liam to see the proof of the lives I took when he learned who I was. But because *I* wanted proof of the lives I took, too.

Proof that I wasn't the same man I once was. That I'd never be him again.

"Gideon," she exhaled, swallowing hard. Then she removed her hand from my torso, bringing them both to my face. Her hold on me was unyielding as she crushed her mouth against mine, pouring every emotion she had into the kiss.

This was one of the things I loved about Imogene, why I fell for her so hard and fast all those years ago. She was incredibly empathetic, something I constantly cited to her as proof that she wasn't, and never could be, like her father. When someone felt pain, she did, too.

And when I felt the warmth of her tears dotting my cheeks, any apprehension about allowing her to see these scars vanished. It was entirely possible I'd regret this later, but right now, right here, I was desperate to experience the human connection I'd been deprived of for years.

Imogene gradually pulled out of the kiss, but didn't look away from my eyes. Not yet. Instead, she wrapped her arms around me, pulling me against her, chest to chest.

I squeezed my eyes shut, relishing in the warmth of her skin against mine as her hands roamed over me. Each touch sent a mixture of desire and longing through me, emotion welling in my throat.

"Was this because of the car accident, too?" she asked softly, as she brushed the flesh along my bicep.

"Broken glass."

She pressed a soft kiss to the angry scar.

"And here?" She caressed a patch of reddened skin along my collarbone.

"Burn marks."

Without a hint of disgust or hesitation, she peppered several affectionate kisses from one side of my collarbone to the other before meeting my eyes once more. Then her attention dropped to one of the most prominent scars on my body.

"And here?" She swallowed hard, her fingers stopping along the jagged line stretching from just below my ribcage to my hipbone. "Still the car accident?"

I nodded. "Puncture wounds."

I'd practiced this story so many times, yet the words felt wrong as they left my mouth. But what could I tell her?

That most of these scars were the result of four years' worth of beatings, torture, and death match fights in the underground prison I'd found myself in after the man who I thought was a good Samaritan turned out to be anything but.

That the scar on my arm was from using the first sharp object I found after my escape to cut off the number branded on me.

That the marred flesh by my clavicle was from being burned with a blow torch.

That the jagged scar along my hipbone was a result of subpar medical care I endured to heal the gunshot wound I suffered when my best friend decided he wanted me dead.

I doubted she'd believe me.

Most days, *I* didn't even believe me.

She continued to trace her fingers over each scar, as if imprinting them to memory. As she continued analyzing my body, I feared some of my old scars would jog her memory. That she'd recognize the mark below my ribcage where one of my foster brothers burned me with a cigarette. Or the freckle above my hipbone. Or the shape of my belly button.

Instead, she simply murmured, "Beautiful."

"Beautiful?" I replied, my voice heavy with emotion. "You find my scars beautiful?"

"I do." She hooked her arm around my neck, forcing my mouth toward hers. "It means you survived when the odds were against you. If you ask me, there's nothing more beautiful than that."

Clutching her face, I crushed my lips to hers, moaning into her as she ran her hands up and down my back, following the lines of even more scars. I stepped out of my shoes, only releasing my hold on her long enough to shove my jeans and boxer briefs down my legs before placing my hand on her back and carefully lowering her onto the mattress.

I settled between her thighs and pulsed against her, groaning at the feel of her heat against my erection. The temptation to push inside of her without a condom was so damn strong. I wanted to. Didn't want anything separating us.

It was bad enough I was sleeping with her, though. I couldn't take any more risks than I already was.

I broke my lips away from hers and grabbed the condom, rolling it on. I teased her with my arousal, spreading her slickness around before slowly easing inside her.

There were no hard thrusts. No punishing drives.

Instead, I took my time, my eyes glued to hers as I watched our bodies join together, inch by incredible inch.

"Fuck," I hissed when I was fully seated.

Her body fit mine perfectly, like two pieces of a puzzle finally reunited.

"Please, Gideon," she begged. "I need you to move or I'm going to lose my goddamn mind." She wrapped her legs around my waist to encourage me to pick up my pace, but I couldn't. Not yet.

"Let me stay here. Let me feel how damn incredible you are. How warm you are." I peppered kisses along her jawline, taking her earlobe between my teeth. "How beautiful you are."

She sighed, running her fingers up and down my back, continuing to follow the lines of my scars.

As the building pressure threatened to overwhelm

me, I shifted inside her, keeping my pace slow and measured. It was a complete change from the way I fucked her during her party. Regardless, she was just as responsive to the gentle rocking of my hips as she was when I was slamming my cock inside of her.

"It's too much," she whimpered, clinging onto me as if I were the only thing keeping her grounded. "Too damn much."

"There's no such thing when it comes to you. With you, it'll never be enough."

She pulled me closer, her uneven breaths fanning over my skin as she pulsed against me. I could tell she was getting close, that she was on the brink of oblivion.

"Do you need me to—"

"No," she answered before I could finish asking if she wanted me to wrap my hand around her throat. "Not this time. I want to stay in the moment." Her eyes locked onto mine with a fierce intensity. "Want to stay with you."

I picked up my pace, and she tightened the hold her legs had around my waist, the two of us moving in perfect harmony together.

The second I felt her clench around me, I slammed my mouth to hers, swallowing her cries as my entire body quaked through my own release. But even once all my tremors subsided, I didn't stop kissing her. And she didn't stop kissing me, the two of us exploring each other as if it were the first time.

And that was what this felt like. Like it *was* the first time. Like I was finally letting her see all of me.

When I finally brought the kiss to an end and peered into her eyes, I prayed I wouldn't see the same thing I did the other night.

Fear.

Panic.

Shame.

"Are you okay?" I asked guardedly. "Are *we* okay?"

She pressed a hand to my cheek, touching her mouth to mine in a soft kiss. "Better than okay." She hesitated, biting her lower lip. "Except..."

"Yes?" I asked, unease creeping in.

"Well, I *was* planning to take a nap." She playfully pouted. "Unfortunately, someone decided he just *had* to stick his dick in me, so those plans are shot to hell."

Laughing, I rolled onto my side, pulling her into my arms. "I didn't hear any complaints from you."

"And you won't. No regrets."

I pressed a soft kiss to her nose. "No regrets."

"No regrets," she confirmed.

Although I had a feeling once she learned the truth, she'd regret everything about this.

CHAPTER TWENTY-FOUR

Gideon

A sea of women in designer dresses and men in tuxedos surrounded me as I entered the ballroom, a server in coattails and white gloves offering me a glass of champagne from his silver tray. I gave him a nod of thanks as I took one before continuing farther into the lavish space.

Crystal chandeliers hung from the ceiling, soft melodies from a string quartet adding to the elegant ambience. Dozens of servers floated gracefully through the room, carrying trays of *hors d'oeuvres*. Several high-top tables were set up near the bar for guests to mingle and enjoy their drinks. Along one wall, a handful of rectangular tables displayed various items for a silent auction, tempting attendees with luxurious one-of-a-kind prizes.

As I expected, I didn't know most of the people here. Despite this weekend benefiting the charity I'd founded, Liam seemed to have forgotten about many of the board members and volunteers who worked tirelessly to make sure kids in similar situations as me didn't end up on the streets or turning to a life of crime.

Instead, the majority of the attendees had a certain social status Liam coveted.

As I walked farther into the room, I spied Melanie at one of the high-top tables with her parents and started toward her, figuring Imogene wasn't too far away.

But as I passed an easel displaying a large portrait, I froze in my tracks.

I came into this weekend fully aware I would come face-to-face with people from my past. I hadn't expected to come face-to-face with my old self.

After escaping my hellish prison and enduring various reconstructive surgeries on my face to repair years' worth of damage, looking into a mirror had been a struggle. At least in those early days. I felt like I was staring at a stranger.

Now, as I studied the portrait of the person I used to be, I felt the same way. Like I was looking at a stranger.

His vibrant smile seemed to mock me with his happiness, his eyes filled with a life and joy I could no longer recognize within myself. He exuded a carefree ease, one I could only dream of having again. It was almost surreal to see him — *me*.

As if I didn't have a care in the world.

As if my former best friend wasn't already planning how to dispose of me, all for the almighty dollar.

"That's Samuel Tate."

I tore my gaze away from the portrait, my pulse kicking up at how stunning Imogene looked in her long, black formal gown, her blonde waves cascading down to her midback.

"He died, correct?" I asked, playing dumb since she hadn't yet shared anything about Samuel with me.

"He was shot by a kid he'd been mentoring." She fully faced me. "Samuel grew up in the foster care system. While some kids have a great experience and end up having a better childhood than they ever could have with their birth parents, that wasn't the case with Samuel. He shared some of the things he endured..." She visibly shivered, tears welling in her eyes once more. She took a moment to collect herself.

"Suffice it to say, he had a rough childhood. Had anger issues. Until someone took him under his wing and taught him martial arts. He once told me that martial arts wasn't about learning how to fight. It was more about learning control and discipline. It saved his life. Allowed him to go to college on a wrestling scholarship and earn a degree in computer programming. That alone changed everything for him, especially when the gaming platform he'd developed with Liam took off. After that, he used his newfound wealth to start a program like the one that saved his life."

"He's the one, isn't he?" I asked after a beat.

She darted her eyes to mine. "What do you mean?"

I narrowed my gaze at her, dropping my voice. "Earlier, you said you hadn't been with anyone who meant something to you in quite a few years. It was him, wasn't it?" I nodded toward the portrait. "The man who meant something?"

"He still *does* mean something to me. If that upsets you, I apologize," she added quickly. "He *is* a part of my past. Always will be. But I'm trying to stop living in my past."

"That's all I care about. I promised to be patient. I'm a man of my word." I took her hand in mine and brought it to my lips, touching a soft kiss to the skin.

It was an innocent gesture, something most people wouldn't think a big deal. But for Imogene, I knew it was a huge step, considering Liam was here.

When we were together all those years ago, she purposefully avoided touching me in his presence for fear of upsetting him. It was why she insisted on keeping our relationship a secret. Granted, I also wanted to keep it from him in the beginning.

Toward the end, I no longer cared about how he might react. All I cared about was finally being able to tell the world how much I loved Imogene.

I'd underestimated the hold he had on her, the blame she'd placed on her shoulders because of what her sperm donor had done to Liam's mother. It didn't matter how many times I'd tried to make her realize that Liam was using that to manipulate her. She refused to see it.

Maybe she finally had.

"Come on. Everyone's over here."

Linking her fingers with mine, she led me toward a high-top table where Melanie and their parents stood, everyone in formal dress. Although I could sense Imogene's stepfather hated everything about the tuxedo he was currently wearing. It was nice to know he was still much more comfortable in a t-shirt and board shorts, even all these years later.

As we approached, Melanie zeroed in on Imogene's hand wrapped in mine and arched a brow. Imogene responded with a small shrug, biting her lower lip.

"Mama, Lachlan, you remember Gideon Saint." She withdrew her hand, allowing me to shake her stepfather's hand.

"Nice to see you again," Lachlan said.

"You, too." I turned from him and touched a chaste kiss to her mother's cheek. "Ms. Hale."

"You can just call me Julia," she admonished.

"Julia." I returned her cordial smile, then faced Melanie and her parents. "Good to see you all."

"Did you have a nice afternoon?" Olivia asked.

"It was quite...refreshing," I responded as I placed my hand on Imogene's hip, pulling her close.

Thankfully, she didn't shrug out of my touch. If anything, she leaned into it.

"Did you go to the driving range with Liam and the others?" Alexander inquired, bringing a rocks glass containing a dark amber liquid to his mouth. "I understand you're playing on their foursome tomorrow."

"Not this time."

"Pretty sure he was more interested in another kind of driving range," Melanie mumbled under her breath from beside Imogene, which earned her daggers from her friend before she nervously glanced at Julia and Lachlan. The room was filled with too much conversation for anyone to have heard, though.

"I figure I'll have my fill of golf tomorrow," I continued. "I've got eighteen excruciating holes to work on my drive."

"I'll drink to that." Lachlan raised his scotch toward me and we clinked glasses.

"So, Gideon," Alexander began after I'd taken a sip of my champagne. "What is it you do?"

"A bit of everything. Lately, my focus has been investments."

"Then I suppose you and Alton will have a lot to talk about tomorrow. Liam and James, too, since the stock market is all those three seem to discuss."

"Not that kind of investment," I corrected. "I prefer to invest in people rather than stocks."

"You do?" Julia tilted her head.

"Yes. Although it's not as altruistic as I make it sound. I own a venture capital firm. Established companies who hope to take their organizations to the next level give me a percentage in exchange for more capital."

"Do you only work with well-established companies?" Lachlan asked.

"Not necessarily. There have been a few ideas I invested in early on as an angel investor. It's still too early to see if it's been a good decision, but I'm hopeful. I like to think I have a good sense for what kind of products or services will be in demand."

"That's like what InvoTech did for Liam and Samuel," Imogene piped up. "They knew they were onto something with their gaming concept, but every bank they went to turned them down since they didn't have much in collateral, apart from a good idea."

"If you ask me, having a good idea is enough collateral," I responded.

"How did you get into this sort of thing?" Alexander pushed, eyeing me with skepticism.

"I worked in the corporate world for about a decade

before wanting to do something different," I answered, giving him the story Henry and I devised for this new person I'd become.

And being the computer wiz he was, Henry made sure everything would be supported in any background check someone might run on me.

Particularly Alexander Burnham.

"Where did you go to college?"

"Stanford."

"And before that? Where did you grow up?" He kept his razor sharp attention focused on me, studying every flinch or hesitation.

But I'd practiced for this. Henry had interrogated me under worse conditions to the point I'd actually started to believe the lies I told.

"Arizona. My father was a CPA and my mother was a teacher."

"Any siblings?"

I shook my head. "Only child."

"Do you see your parents often?"

"Dad," Melanie hissed, glaring at him. "Stop interrogating the poor guy."

"It's okay. He just wants to make sure I'm who I say I am." I turned back to Alexander. "Unfortunately, the only time I get to see my parents these days is when I visit their graves."

Olivia touched a hand to her chest, sympathy

swirling in her dark eyes. "I'm so sorry to hear that." She gently nudged Alexander. The heated look she gave silently berated him to play nice. "My condolences."

"It happened a long time ago. Car accident."

She briefly closed her eyes. After all, she'd lost her mother the same way.

"But enough about me. I'm probably the least interesting person here." I tore my gaze away from Alexander and addressed Lachlan. "What do you think Atlanta's chances are to go all the way this year?"

"It looks to be a solid team, although it's still early," he answered, everyone shifting their attention to him.

Everyone except for Alexander, who kept his eyes focused intently on me.

CHAPTER TWENTY-FIVE

Imogene

"He's quite handsome, isn't he?" Mama remarked later in the evening as we sat at our table alone.

Liam had gone to smoke a cigar with Alton and James, Melanie and Olivia had disappeared to the ladies' room, and Alexander and Lachlan had snuck off to the lobby bar to check the score of the game.

That was over a half-hour ago now.

I couldn't blame them. I'd much rather watch a baseball game at the bar than be in here surrounded by a bunch of people I had absolutely nothing in common with.

"Who's that?"

I tore my eyes away from Gideon as he sat at his table, seemingly in deep conversation with a few of the octogenarian women Liam placed him with — the mother of some oil tycoon, a horse breeder, and an eccentric heiress who acquired an entire hotel chain when her husband died. I was pretty sure the wealth in this room alone was higher than the GDP of several small countries.

"You know who I'm talking about," Mama replied in a low voice, leaning closer. "Mr. Gideon Saint."

I took a sip of my wine in an attempt to ignore the heat washing over my face from the mention of him. It was a losing battle, especially when he glanced my way, a soft smile curving his lips. He looked so effortlessly handsome and confident, even among all these wealthy individuals.

Then again, he was extremely wealthy himself. But he didn't flaunt it like most everyone else here did.

"Ah, young love," Mama teased, a mischievous twinkle in her eye.

"It's not like that."

She arched a brow. "It sure looks that way. You may not have noticed, but all throughout dinner, he kept glancing in your direction."

Oh, I definitely noticed. To be fair, I was surprised he wasn't sitting with us to begin with. Liam explained since Gideon was a last-minute addition, he had his assistant put him wherever there was room.

I knew it was a bullshit response, considering

Mitchell, the person Gideon had replaced in their four-some, was originally at our table. Liam just didn't want him anywhere near me if he could help it.

"So tell me." Mama leaned closer, her eyes sparkling with excitement. "What's going on with you two?"

If she'd asked me earlier, I would have told her nothing *was* going on. That wasn't the case now. Not anymore.

"We're taking it slow. Figuring out if there's something there."

Mama pushed out a sigh of relief as she wrapped an arm around my shoulders. "It's about time you got back out there, sweetheart."

I closed my eyes, basking in her embrace. "I know."

"And that you stopped letting the guilt you feel about Liam stand in your way." She dropped her hold on me.

"I don't—"

"Don't get me wrong. I adore Liam. While I questioned your friendship at first, considering your connection, I think you both needed each other. Needed that closure. But I *also* think a lot of your decisions where Liam is concerned are influenced by a certain level of guilt over what happened to his mother."

"I thought you were 'Team Liam'," I said, using air quotes. "Hell, you thought I should move in with him after the incident at the club a few weeks back."

"I never said that," she retorted.

"You didn't?" I scrunched my brow. "He told me he called you. That you thought it was a good idea for me to move in with him."

She shook her head. "That's not what I said at all, Imogene. I simply told him that I was grateful he was nearby to keep an eye on you."

I parted my lips, blinking repeatedly. "He made it sound like you were on board with me moving into his place."

She covered my hand with hers and squeezed. "The only team I'm on is Team Imogene. I know how important it was for you to leave Atlanta. For you to have a fresh start, especially after everything." She briefly glanced at the portrait of Samuel. "Call me crazy, but I don't think you'd get that living with Liam. Plus, I know you…" She pulled her hand from mine and brought her wine glass to her lips. "There's no way you'd move to Southern California and not live within a short walk of the beach."

I chuckled, relaxing back into my chair as couples danced to the jazz ensemble that had replaced the string quartet.

"I can go from my bed to riding a wave in less than ten minutes."

"He may not be your birth father, but Lachlan's influence is written all over you."

"If you ask me, that's a good thing."

"It certainly is." She tilted her drink toward me and we clinked glasses. "You are a sucker for blue eyes, though, aren't you? I almost had to do a double take when I saw him."

"Who?"

"Gideon." She discreetly nodded in his direction. "His eyes are the same shade of blue as Samuel's were. But Gideon's..." She trailed off, pinching her lips together in a tight line. "They're more...haunted, I suppose. Samuel's were full of life. Like every day was a new adventure." She returned her gaze to mine. "Gideon's don't have the same spark."

I hadn't thought about it like that before. All I saw were eyes with the same aqua blue hue as the man I still mourned.

Now that I was able to look between Samuel's portrait and Gideon, the difference was staggering, the thirst Samuel had for life readily apparent. Like Mama said, he viewed every day as a new adventure.

As a gift.

Gideon didn't have that same hunger. He was more hardened, filled with unspoken pain. Maybe that was what had drawn me to his eyes when we first met. Not the similarity, but the darkness within. In many ways, it mirrored my own.

"Regardless, they're still quite sexy." Mama pulled my attention back to her.

"They certainly are."

Especially when he came undone.

I never understood how a pair of eyes could convey such deep and primal craving until I met Gideon. Whenever he looked at me, it was as if he could see every forbidden desire and carnal longing I'd tried to mask for years.

But with him, I didn't have to hide any of those desires. Not anymore.

"Did I miss anything?" Melanie asked when she returned to the table with her mother, plopping down in the seat beside me. "Are the menfolk still at the bar?"

I blew out a laugh. "What do you think?"

"I didn't realize it would take close to an hour to check the score of the game," Olivia remarked.

"Or that it was necessary to go to the bar to begin with," Mama added. "I could be wrong, but cell phones have marvelous capabilities these days, including the ability to check baseball scores without having to be near a television."

"Perhaps we should go look for them," Melanie suggested with a devious glint in her eyes. "They could have gotten lost. And who knows what dangers they may have encountered on their quest. We *are* near Big Sur, after all. Bears have been spotted on occasion."

That was all the invitation Mama and Olivia needed,

both of them jumping to their feet, wavering slightly due to all the wine they'd consumed.

"Then we must save them," Mama said around a laugh. "We'd never forgive ourselves otherwise." She looked my way. "Will you be joining us, too?" She stole a discreet glance toward Gideon.

I hesitated, but he knew where my room was. He could find me later.

I *really* hoped he'd find me later.

"What kind of person would I be if I allowed you all to go off on this dangerous mission alone?" Standing, I finished the last of my wine and grabbed my clutch. I briefly floated my gaze toward the terrace and wondered if I should let Liam know I was leaving.

It wasn't like I was here with him, though. I was here on my own. So I could leave on my own.

Which was exactly what I did, looping my arm through Melanie's as we made our escape and headed toward the lobby lounge.

Not surprising, Lachlan and Alexander stood at the bar, their eyes glued to the television screen, cheering for the Red Sox as if it were the playoffs instead of one of the first games of the season.

Then again, they *were* playing the Yankees. No matter how early in the season, those were important games, a fact I learned from living with Melanie, who was born and raised a diehard Red Sox fan, as she told me.

"Just checking the score of the game?" Olivia crossed her arms in front of her chest, giving Alexander a playful look of disapproval.

"They're playing the Yankees. You can't expect me *not* to watch, love."

"I'm only upset that it took me this long to figure out what you two were doing." She sidled up next to him, and he wrapped his arm around her, kissing the top of her head.

The two men looked infinitely more comfortable now that they'd removed their ties, vests, and jackets, the top button of their crisp shirts undone, their sleeves rolled up.

"In our defense, it did go into extra innings," Lachlan added, gesturing to the TV, the broadcast indicating it was currently the top of the eleventh.

"Then I guess that means we need some drinks," Mama suggested, signaling the bartender.

I was about to order an old fashioned when I noticed a familiar silhouette approach the bank of elevators. Gideon stood tall and imposing, his sharp jawline and intense gaze sending shivers down my spine. Mama followed my line of sight, giving me an encouraging look.

"On second thought..." I smoothed a hand down my

black dress. "I'm pretty tired. I think I'll call it a night and get some rest."

"Right...," Melanie drew out, glancing toward Gideon. "You go rest." She gave me an exaggerated wink.

I playfully swatted her.

"Have a good evening, sweetie." Mama squeezed me tightly. "And have fun," she whispered.

I wasn't sure whether to be embarrassed or grateful I had a mom who supported what I planned to do tonight.

And it wasn't sleep.

After I said a quick goodbye to everyone, promising to meet them for breakfast, I started in Gideon's direction.

The air crackled with electricity as I approached, my pulse quickening with every step. It had only been a few hours since his hands had been on my body, but it felt like an eternity.

"Ms. Prescott," he greeted smoothly.

"Mr. Saint," I replied in a flirtatious tone. "I hope you enjoyed your evening."

"I did." He narrowed his gaze at me. "Not as much as I enjoyed my afternoon, though. I found my company during dinner somewhat lacking."

"I'm sorry to hear that. I do hope your luck changes and the rest of your evening is much more...enjoyable."

His jaw ticked as it always did whenever he struggled to control himself. "Oh, I'm counting on that, Ms. Prescott."

I bit my lower lip, the way he looked at me causing moisture to pool between my thighs. It didn't help I wasn't wearing any panties. Not because it was a slim-fitting dress, as was the case at my birthday party.

But because I knew it drove Gideon wild.

"After you," Gideon said when the elevator doors slid open, allowing me to enter in front of him.

The doors hadn't even been closed for a second before he looped an arm around me, tugging me against his hard and firm body.

"About that change of luck..."

Then he slammed his mouth against mine.

CHAPTER TWENTY-SIX

Gideon

"How did I go so long without this?" Imogene struggled to catch her breath as she clung to me, her body still trembling from the orgasm I just treated her to.

The sunlight streamed in through the window, casting a warm glow over her flushed cheeks and tousled hair, her lips swollen and skin slick with sweat.

I hadn't expected her to knock on my door this morning. I'd left her less than an hour ago so she could have breakfast with her parents while I got ready for today's tournament. I'd barely had the door cracked open to ask what she was doing here when she pushed her way inside and slammed her lips against mine.

She was impossible to resist.

Especially when I dragged my hand up her leg and learned she hadn't been wearing any panties underneath her sundress.

It made me even more desperate to have her.

In a flash, my plans for the morning went out the window, like check in with Henry to make sure everything for today was still proceeding as planned.

With Imogene's body against mine, all my worries disappeared, my only thought that of losing myself in her.

"I don't know," I replied, covering her mouth with mine. "But I'll do everything to make sure you don't go too long without a good fucking again."

"You'd take that upon yourself?" She smirked, running her fingers through my hair.

"It might be a difficult job, but I think I've proven I'm up for the challenge."

When I slowly circled my hips to drive the point home, she threw her head back, her infectious laughter filling the room.

God, I loved that sound. Loved seeing her carefree and happy. Loved knowing *I* made her feel carefree and happy.

Even if I'd eventually be the one to shatter that happiness.

"I do believe you have." She pulled my lips back to hers. "But first, you need to get down to the golf course."

I groaned and buried my face in the crook of her neck. "Can't I just stay here and fuck you all day? I'd much rather go eighteen rounds with you."

She swatted me away. "Fiend."

"What can I say?" I waggled my brows as I pulled out of her, stepping away from the desk I'd placed her on in my desperate rush to feel her. "You've turned me into an addict." I pressed a kiss to her lips, our tongues briefly tangling. "But if you insist I spend my day playing this dreadful sport instead of fucking you, I'll oblige. Just promise me one thing."

"What's that?"

I leaned my forehead against hers. "You. Me. Dinner. Tonight. Alone."

"I think that can be arranged."

"Good." Touching one last kiss to her mouth, I excused myself to the bathroom, taking a moment to clean up and get dressed.

When I stepped back into the living room of my suite, Imogene had smoothed her hair and was applying a touch of gloss to her lips. I approached her from behind and pulled her against me, skimming my mouth against her neck.

"If you ask me, you don't need any makeup. You're perfect just the way you are."

She closed her eyes, drawing in a shaky breath. "You really shouldn't say those things to me."

"Why? It's true."

She faced me, draping an arm over my shoulder. "Because then I might just take you up on your offer to go eighteen rounds with me instead."

"Why the hell did I agree to play golf?" I ground out.

"Because it's for a good cause. And besides…" She inched her lips toward mine. "Sometimes delayed gratification can be infinitely more satisfying." She lingered near my mouth for a beat, the promise of her kiss within reach.

Then she spun around, opening the door and stepping into the hallway.

When I didn't immediately follow, she arched a brow. "Are you coming?'

"I wish I were," I muttered under my breath as I joined her, placing my hand on her lower back and guiding her toward the bank of elevators.

As we waited for one to arrive, I pulled her against me, unable to stop touching her. Especially since I was about to go all day without her. The thought sounded like torture now, despite the fact I went years without her.

Hell, for the past several months, I hated her.

That all changed yesterday when I showed her my scars and she didn't cringe. Didn't get disgusted.

Instead, she called them the one thing I never thought anyone would.

She called them beautiful, a testament to my strength.

"I just can't get enough of this body." I trailed my hand up a leg, lifting the skirt of her dress after confirming no one was nearby. But when I was met with soft material instead of bare flesh, I narrowed my gaze on her.

"How did you get panties?"

"They were in my purse. I took them off on the elevator on my way to your room."

"You better have been alone."

"Why? Jealous?"

"I don't share, Imogene."

"Good to know." She pushed away from me as the elevator doors opened. "Come on. Time to golf."

"I'd rather fuck," I reminded her, reluctantly stepping onto the elevator. "The only hole-in-one I'm interested is the one between your legs."

Once the doors closed, giving us one last moment of privacy, I pulled her toward me, squeezing her ass.

"Or maybe this one." I teased her crack as I dragged my tongue along the column of her neck, praying the elevator didn't stop on any of the other floors. "Has anyone ever fucked you here before?"

"N-No." Her response came out breathy. Wanton.

"Have you thought about doing that?" I nipped at

her skin, feeling her body tighten under me, her chest rising and falling in an increased rhythm.

"Y-yes."

"It turns you on, doesn't it? The idea of my cock fucking your tight hole?"

I pressed harder against her so she could feel how much it turned me on, too.

"God, yes." Her eyes fluttered closed as I teased her for another second.

"And I will." I pulled back, putting as much space between us as possible, if for no other reason than to give my hard-on a moment to go down.

As the elevator slowed to a stop, I stole a glance her way, her complexion flushed. Exactly how I wanted her — eager and wanting.

"But first things first..."

I extended my arm, allowing her to exit before me, which she did on shaky legs. Returning my hand to the small of her back, I steered her through the lobby and out toward the golf course, the place abuzz with activity.

"Remember what I said yesterday..." I leaned closer, keeping my voice low. "I own all your orgasms. No getting yourself off without me today."

She briefly squeezed her eyes shut, her fists balling in frustration. "Today's going to be a long fucking day," she breathed.

"You've got that right," I responded as we approached the green.

"There you are!" Liam exclaimed when he saw me. "I was beginning to wonder if..." He trailed off, noticing Imogene at my side.

"My apologies. I had some unexpected business come up this morning that required my undivided attention." I gazed at Imogene with nothing short of affection.

It was obvious Liam picked up my not-so-subtle innuendo, his jaw tensing, nostrils flaring.

Imogene averted her gaze as she fidgeted with the hem of her dress, obviously uncomfortable with my insinuation. But this *was* part of the reason I wanted to involve Imogene in the beginning.

Even if it was no longer the only reason I was spending time with her.

"Shall we?" I said in a chipper voice. "Don't want to keep you waiting any longer."

"Of course." Liam gritted a smile, playing the part of the gracious host.

Little did he know, in mere hours, his world would start unraveling around him.

And I would have a front-row seat.

CHAPTER TWENTY-SEVEN

Gideon

"Is this your first time golfing Pebble Beach?" James asked later in the morning as we walked from the golf cart to the tee, surrounded by lush greenery and the smell of freshly cut grass. The sun beat down on us, but due to our proximity to the ocean, there was still a slight chill in the air.

"Actually, yes." I leaned closer, as if about to reveal a secret. "In case you haven't noticed, I'm not that great of a golfer."

He raised an eyebrow, a playful glint in his eye. "You don't say."

"True story."

He chuckled, flashing that politician's smile he'd perfected. "Then I'll let *you* in on a little secret."

"What's that?"

"It's not my favorite sport, either."

"Is that right?"

"Unfortunately, in my line of work, it's a necessary evil. Can't broker deals and move up the ladder without spending time on the golf course." He took a long drag from his beer.

"At least it's for a good cause," I said, if for no other reason than to gauge his reaction.

This was why I'd jumped at the opportunity to join their foursome when it presented itself. To get close to the men responsible for what happened to me. Earn their trust.

Then use that trust against them.

Much like they'd used *my* trust against me.

"It certainly is," James agreed.

"This charity," I continued, following him toward the tee. "It was his friend's charity that he continued in his honor, correct?" I gestured toward Liam as he took a club from his caddy.

I knew the answer. I wanted to hear *his* answer. See how he reacted. Hell, I wanted to see how they all reacted.

"He did."

"Samuel Tate, right?"

At the sound of the name — my old name — a hush

fell over the group, the three men looking around at each other, like the co-conspirators they were.

"That's right," Liam answered before lining up his shot, pulling back and swinging.

"You were all close with him?"

"Liam knew him the best," Alton explained. "Met when they were teens at a program much like the one this tournament benefits. They were even roommates for a time while they developed their gaming platform."

"Cloud Hero, right?"

"People thought we were crazy," Liam remarked. "Said no one would be interested in a platform that allowed users to create their own games in a simulated world." He rolled his eyes. "Guess they were all wrong."

"Guess they were." I allowed a brief silence to pass, not wanting to seem too eager. Then I asked, "How did he die?"

All their expressions turned wary, and I inhaled sharply, pretending to realize my mistake.

"My apologies," I said quickly. "I don't mean to pry. I'm just curious after hearing bits and pieces about him and why this charity was important to him."

"He was shot," Liam answered.

"My god. That must have been difficult for you. To lose a friend and a business partner." I shifted my gaze toward Alton and James. "All of you."

"It certainly was." Liam swallowed hard, feigning grief.

I knew the truth, though.

This man didn't grieve me for a single moment over the past several years.

Not when my being out of the picture cleared the path for him to get exactly what he wanted. Allowed him to sell out to a huge media company that went against everything we stood for.

At least everything I *thought* we stood for.

I should have known Liam would change his mind when billions of dollars were dangled in front of him like a juicy steak.

"Those first few months were especially tough in," Liam continued. "I lost count of how many times I reached for my phone to text him, or went to his office whenever I had an idea, only to remember he wasn't here anymore. That's why I decided to sell Cloud Hero in the end."

I had to hand it to him. He was a damn good liar. Then again, he'd had five years to perfect his story. Make himself sound like he sold our platform to ImageScape because he grieved my loss. Not because of the huge payday or the fact he was given a position on the board.

"Did they ever catch the guy who did it?"

"Sure did," James boasted. "It wasn't easy, though, since it was hard to prove murder without a body."

I widened my eyes. "There was no body?"

James shook his head. "Nope. And to this day, it still hasn't been found. Thankfully, there was enough blood left behind to rule it a homicide, especially considering the high crime area it was found in."

"Then—"

"Sam worked with a lot of troubled kids. The police arrested one of them for it. I was the prosecuting attorney on the case."

"Wouldn't that be a conflict of interest, considering your ties?"

He shrugged. "I wasn't as close to him as Liam and Alton. But I promised Liam I'd make sure justice was served."

I sipped on my beer, my grip on the bottle tightening as I fought the urge to strangle all three of these bastards for what they did to Jonah. He'd turned his life around. Was planning to go to college. Only for these fuckers to frame him for a murder he had nothing to do with. He wasn't even given the opportunity to mount a defense, not when, within days of his arrest, he was the victim of a brutal assault that left him brain dead.

His mother was forced to make the decision no parent should. Jonah went to his grave with the world thinking he was a murderer.

Whenever I questioned whether this was the right path, I reminded myself I wasn't the only one they wronged. Jonah was as much of a victim as me. I needed to do this for him.

For his poor mother.

"Well, I'm glad you all got the justice you deserved. That *Samuel* got the justice he deserved."

"He certainly did," Liam responded just as a buzzing sounded. He reached into his pocket and retrieved his cell. "Speaking of justice, this is the detective looking into Imogene's attack. Excuse me for a moment."

I kept my expression even, fighting against the grin begging to be set free at how much of a turn Liam's day was about to take.

How much of a turn it was about to take for all of them.

"Who's up?" Alton took a long swig from his beer. "Is it you?"

"I believe so," I responded, grabbing the club my caddy handed me before lining up at the tee.

The entire time, I kept Liam in my sights. His body was turned away, but I could see his irritation and frustration from several yards away.

No doubt Detective Wheeler was currently informing him about the break they'd had in the case — that Benjamin Astor's body had finally been discovered with a fatal gunshot wound to his abdomen.

But that wasn't all.

He'd also inform him they'd found the body on

Liam's sailboat after a concerned member of the marina noticed an unusual odor emanating from it.

I adjusted my stance and swung the club, a sense of vindication filling me as I made contact with the ball, sending it sailing toward the green.

One thing was certain.

After today, Liam's life as he knew it would soon come to an end.

And I couldn't wait to watch him go down in flames.

CHAPTER TWENTY-EIGHT

Gideon

"I see you survived without too much injury," Lachlan greeted when I joined him and Alexander in the lobby lounge later in the day.

As expected, Liam had been noticeably distracted after Detective Wheeler's phone call. His usually confident and easygoing demeanor had been replaced with a tense, nervous energy, so much so that he played worse than I did, and that was saying something. I couldn't help but find satisfaction in watching him slowly unravel as he learned exactly how it felt to be accused of a crime he didn't commit.

Throughout the afternoon, he'd made quite a few calls himself, probably to his legal team. I had no doubt they'd work tirelessly to clear his name. After all, *he* didn't kill Benjamin Astor.

I did.

That didn't mean I couldn't enjoy watching Liam sweat a little right now. I wasn't sure what worried him more — the potential of facing murder charges, or the possibility that Imogene might find out he was the one who'd paid Benjamin to send her those necklaces in the first place.

"No physical scars, but it might take a few days to get over the mental anguish," I answered.

Lachlan threw his head back and laughed, raising his drink to his lips. "Same here."

I looked from him to Alexander, who continued to watch me with suspicion. "How was your day, sir?"

"Only managed to hit the ball in the rough twice, so I'd say it was a win."

"Good to hear." I gave him a small smile just as my phone buzzed in my pocket.

I pulled it out and opened the text.

HENRY:

Headline should hit in the next five minutes.

I briefly scanned the lounge, finding Alton shamelessly flirting with one of the cocktail waitresses. He'd been doing the same thing all day, relentlessly hitting on the women working the bar cart whenever it drove by. I could see the irritation and annoyance on their faces grow with each passing encounter, which got worse the more he drank. I'd tried to encourage him to tone it down, but he brushed it off, claiming the girls had no choice but to put up with it if they wanted to keep their job.

If I had any doubts about whether I was doing the right thing, spending the past several hours with these assholes eviscerated them. I thought I might see a hint of the men I once knew.

I didn't.

They'd all allowed money and power to turn them into people I barely recognized.

ME:

Looking forward to it.

HENRY:

How's Liam?

ME:

Inwardly shitting bricks, I'd presume. Once he received that phone call, he was distracted.

He's still typing frantically on his phone, probably making sure there aren't any reports about him being a person of interest in a murder investigation.

HENRY:

He's not the one who has to worry
about a headline. Not yet anyway.

"Everything okay?" Alexander asked, pulling my attention back to him.

"Just an issue at work. As much as I love the convenience of these things..." I waved my phone before tucking it back into my pocket, "they can be a curse, especially when you're always supposed to be within reach."

"That's one of the reasons I love surfing," Lachlan interjected. "No cell phones. No technology. Nothing. The only thing you're connected with is the ocean and nature. It's incredibly liberating."

"I'd like to try it some time."

"You should."

"So what's going—"

The sound of glass shattering against the floor interrupted Alexander's question, causing a hush to descend over the lobby as everyone turned toward the source.

Alton stood frozen in place, his eyes glued to his phone. Mine vibrated in my pocket and I retrieved it to see the notification from a top newspaper flash on my home screen.

CEO of GeoCom Industries alleged to have been involved in several instances of sexual misconduct

"Alton..." James gritted out, standing from the leather couch and approaching his friend. "People are staring. What's going on?"

Alton shook his head, panic covering every inch of him. Maybe even a hint of disbelief. As if he'd blink and it would all be a bad dream.

I knew that feeling all too well.

I'd prayed for that very thing every day for years. Prayed I'd wake up and learn the hell I'd been living was merely a product of my imagination.

Now he knew how it felt.

And this was only the beginning.

"I..." Alton's hand flew up to his chest as he struggled to breathe. "GeoCom. It... I..." His gaze locked on mine, wild with desperation and anger. "You." He stormed toward me.

I jumped to my feet, holding my hands defensively in front of me. I could have easily punched him. Had him on the ground in a heartbeat. But I didn't need to raise anyone's suspicions unnecessarily.

"You did this," he seethed, his voice dripping with venom.

"Did what?" I kept my tone even, my demeanor calm, bordering on indifferent.

"This." He thrust his phone toward me, the headline glaring in bold letters.

"How would I have anything to do with that?"

"You misled me. Made me think the merger was a done deal."

"Merger?" I feigned confusion. "I don't..." I trailed off, acting as if I finally put the pieces together, even though this was the plan all along. "The file?" I leaned closer. "You looked at it?"

"You left the papers all over your desk."

I scrunched my brows, concern filling my voice. "Did you...use that information?"

"I—"

"Alton." James' warning interrupted him, stopping him from incriminating himself any further, especially in a room full of witnesses. "I think it might be best if you went upstairs."

Alton clenched his jaw, looking like he was on the verge of breaking into tears. Liam appeared panicked, too. They all did. No doubt they all used the supposedly ironclad information Alton gave them to make some big trades in their portfolio.

And if everything went as predicted, when the markets opened Monday morning, those portfolios would be worth substantially less.

They'd bought up stock in GeoCom thinking it would soon be acquiring TechAway, the company responsible for revolutionizing smart home systems across the world. While the draft press release Alton had seen *was* legit, as someone who owned fourteen percent of TechAway, I thought it best to make sure it would be a good fit.

On paper, it was.

But when I had Henry put his impeccable hacking skills to use, I learned GeoCom's executive board had more skeletons in its closet than a graveyard.

It wasn't my fault Alton failed to read the minutes from the board of directors meeting where we unanimously voted *not* to accept GeoCom's offer, that he'd acted on insider information in obvious violation of securities law.

Nor was it my fault that both Liam and James also hoped to use that information to increase their bank accounts.

Regardless, I was going to enjoy every second of watching their carefully constructed house of cards slowly crumble around them. There was nothing they could do to stop it.

Alton's angry gaze seared into mine, his body tense and coiled like a snake ready to strike. I could see the battle raging within — wanting to release some of his aggression on me, but also knowing he needed to minimize any further damage to his career and reputation.

In just a few days, he wouldn't have either.

"Come on," James encouraged, attempting to pull him away.

Finally, Alton released a sigh and shuffled away, James and Liam following close behind. But before Liam disappeared into the elevator, he threw me a heated glare laced with suspicion.

"What was that about?" Alexander asked once everyone returned to their conversations.

Although the conversation now seemed to be about what could have upset easygoing, congenial Alton Sinclair.

"Earlier this week, I met with Alton to discuss him handling a few of my investments. It appears he took a peek at a confidential file and made some insider trades based on the information he gleaned without seeing the full picture. News just broke that, in all likelihood, is about to have a disastrous effect on the stocks I assume he bought."

Alexander shook his head in disapproval. "It's about time he finally got caught."

Yes, it is, I thought to myself.

CHAPTER TWENTY-NINE

Imogene

I checked my reflection in the full-length mirror, hoping the one-shoulder black dress would be adequate for wherever Gideon planned to take me tonight. He hadn't told me and I worried I'd be either underdressed or overdressed, so I tried to find something that could go either way. The dress was sexy, landing at my mid-thigh, but the straight cut and flowing material along one sleeve gave it a casual feel, too.

And then there was the big question — whether to wear panties.

I opted for no panties.

It was risqué, but it drove Gideon wild. I did stuff a pair in my purse, just in case.

A knock on the door jolted me out of my fantasy

about Gideon sliding his hand between my legs in a busy restaurant.

After one last look at my appearance, I grabbed my purse and opened the door, expecting to see a tall, dark, and handsome man on the other side.

Instead, Liam stood in the hallway, his hair disheveled, his polo shirt untucked from his khaki pants. He was normally calm and collected. Not tonight.

"Where are you going?" he barked in an accusatory tone.

"To dinner."

"With who? I just bumped into your parents. They said they were staying in tonight."

"They are." I held my head high. "I'm going out with Gideon."

"What's going on with you two?" he snapped, his hands forming into fists. "Are you letting him fuck you?"

"I'm not *letting* him do anything, Liam. Even if I were, it's none of your business."

"The hell it isn't!" he roared. I caught a whiff of alcohol on his breath, the stench pungent.

"Liam," I warned, remaining on alert.

He'd never put a hand on me before, but something about him was different tonight.

"Shit, Gin..." He hung his head, the weight of regret etched into his features. When he returned his gaze to mine, the old Liam was back, his expression softening.

"I'm sorry." He grabbed my hand and traced gentle circles along my knuckles with his thumb.

"It's just... I can't quite put my finger on it, but there's something...off about him. I don't trust him. Not for a fucking second."

"And yet you let him play in your golf tournament?" I pulled my hand from his and crossed my arms in front of my chest, purposefully not inviting him into my room. "And on your foursome, no less?"

"That was more Alton's doing."

"You could have rescinded his invitation. Or were the zeros in his bank account too tempting?"

"It was a strategic move. I wanted to see if I could figure out what he wants from you. Why he seems so interested."

"Because you don't think he'd be interested otherwise?"

"I didn't say that." He grabbed my biceps, smoothing his hands down my arms in a reassuring manner. "I don't want you to get hurt. That's all." He chewed on his lower lip. "Especially considering the timing of everything."

I stepped out of his touch. "What are you talking about?"

"About the necklaces. Then the attack outside the club, where he just so happened to be and was able to intervene. It seems a little too...convenient."

I placed my hands on my hips. "What are you insinuating?"

He gave a noncommittal shrug of his shoulders. "I'm simply stating the obvious, Gin."

"You can't seriously think Gideon was involved. What would his motive be?"

"He *did* kill the guy who attacked you. And Benjamin Astor? The guy who the police believe sent you those necklaces?"

"What about him?"

"His body was found today. On *my* fucking sailboat. Shot in the abdomen."

A chill trickled down my spine. "Who killed him?"

"Hell if I know!" He dropped his voice. "I sure as shit didn't do it. But *someone* did." He curved toward me. "And maybe that person is the man you've been spreading your legs for."

"That's ridiculous." I pushed past him and stormed down the hallway toward the elevators, needing to put as much space between us as possible before I said something I'd regret.

"Then how do you explain this thing with Alton?" he called after me.

I whirled around. "What thing with Alton?"

Liam stepped closer, lowering his voice to a barely audible level. "Alton had a meeting with him earlier in the week and saw a draft press release announcing

GeoCom's acquisition of TechAway. He bought up thousands of shares of GeoCom since he knew an acquisition like this would have a positive impact on their stock price."

"Which is illegal," I reminded him.

Liam waved me off. "Then a few hours ago, a breaking news story hit about the CEO of GeoCom being involved in a huge corporate coverup of sexual assault. It just seems too...convenient. Like he planned it."

"Gideon planned for a CEO to sexually assault dozens of his employees, some quite brutally, as well as bribe officials to cover it up, so he could...what?"

"I don't fucking know, Gin! But between this, the body on my boat, and your attack, there's a lot of suspicious shit going on. And it didn't start until Gideon entered our lives. What the hell is it going to take for you to see that? To open your goddamn eyes!"

"Gideon has *nothing* to do with any of it! You're being ridiculous. He *saved* my life. He's a good person."

"You don't know that! You don't know anything about him!" He threw up his hands in frustration.

"I know he makes me happy. And I know the only reason you're doing this is because you can't *stand* the idea of another man actually being interested. Or worse. That *I'd* be interested in someone other than you. But I'm *not* interested in you, Liam. I never have been. We may have slept together, but it was the biggest fucking mistake of my life. One you can be damn sure I'll never make again. So—"

The shrill sound of a bell echoed through the hallway, and I clamped my mouth shut as the elevator doors opened and Gideon stepped out. When he saw Liam and me, he hesitated, obviously picking up on the heavy tension.

"I'm sorry. I didn't mean to interrupt."

"You didn't." I pinned Liam with a glare, then hurried into the elevator, Gideon following close behind with a protective hand on my back.

"Ginny..." Liam begged, advancing toward me.

"No, Liam," I snapped, cutting him off. "There's no coming back from the things you just said. Not this time." I glowered at him until the door closed between us. Then I exhaled a long breath, falling against the wall.

"Is everything okay?" Gideon asked after a beat.

I swallowed down the lump building in my throat. It wasn't Liam I was upset with, although I was certainly irritated.

I was more upset with myself for not seeing what Melanie had been trying to tell me for years.

What *Samuel* had tried to tell me.

Liam would do anything to keep me as his.

It was sad that it took him accusing an innocent man of murder to make me see that.

"This has been building for a while," I admitted with a sigh. "It was only a matter of time until it blew up."

"What happened?" Gideon swept his concerned gaze over mine. "He didn't hurt you, did he?"

The protective edge in his voice flooded my body with warmth, despite my annoyance with Liam.

"Because I swear to god, Imogene. I don't care if he's your friend, I'll—"

Straightening, I pressed a hand to his chest. "I'm fine," I assured him. "Long story short, he doesn't trust you."

"He probably shouldn't." He flashed a devious smile, the heat in his stare cutting through the tension.

"And why's that?" I playfully waggled my brows.

"Because of all the things I plan to do to you later on." He looped an arm around my waist and dragged my body against his. "I've been making a list all day."

"Well, then..." I played with a few tufts of hair that fell over the collar of his crisp black suit.

I loved this man in black. There was something about the darkness of his clothes that made the blue in his eyes pop even more.

"Why don't we go have some dinner so we can get back and see how many things we can cross off that list?" I murmured, brushing my lips against his.

"I like the sound of that."

CHAPTER THIRTY

Imogene

I moved through my hotel room, doing one final check of the space to make sure I hadn't left anything behind. As luck would have it, I did find a pair of panties when I tossed the sheets. I didn't think I wore panties enough this weekend to leave a pair in the bed. Especially since most of the time I spent in this bed was with Gideon.

And the things we did definitely didn't require panties.

After shoving them in my suitcase, I took one last sip of coffee and was about to toss the cup into the garbage, but paused, my eyes falling on the contents. Particularly the used condom Gideon threw in there this morning.

The argument I had with Liam replayed in my mind.

How I didn't know anything about Gideon. How none of the suspicious shit started happening until he entered the picture.

How maybe *he* was the one behind the necklaces.

But what was I going to do? Take this condom and ask Melanie's dad if he'd have someone at his security company run Gideon's DNA? For what? To see if it matched any DNA they found on the necklaces I'd received?

Or worse, to see if Gideon's DNA matched my ex-boyfriend?

My *dead* ex-boyfriend.

My *dead* ex-boyfriend who looked nothing like Gideon, apart from the eyes.

But even those were missing something, just like my mama said the other night.

Samuel had always radiated an infectious energy, always ready for an adventure at a moment's notice. His mere presence could light up a room.

Gideon was...different. More burdened and haunted. There was a sadness in his eyes and a tension in his shoulders that spoke of a troubled past. It probably had something to do with losing his parents in the car accident that left his body scarred. I'd wanted to ask for more details, but didn't want to spoil our time together.

So what if Gideon did crossword puzzles like

Samuel? Told Ollie to heel like Samuel? Kissed me like Samuel?

He *wasn't* Samuel.

I promised myself I'd stop living in the past. And that was exactly what I would do.

Not to mention the police had already identified the guy who gave me the necklaces, and it wasn't Gideon. While it was certainly troubling that Benjamin Astor's body had been found on Liam's boat, it didn't mean Gideon was involved.

I was just allowing Liam under my skin. I wasn't going to let him. Not anymore. No more doing whatever Liam asked of me simply because of the guilt I felt for the role my sperm donor played in his shitty upbringing.

Without giving the condom or Liam's misplaced concerns a second thought, I collected my things and continued out of my room.

As I stepped into the bustling lobby, I found Lachlan and Mama talking with Melanie and her parents.

"It was so good seeing you again, sweetie." Olivia wrapped me in a hug when I approached. "You'll be up in Boston in a few weeks, correct?"

"The team has a game there in May, I believe."

"Try to clear some time for us, if you can."

"I'm happy to," I assured her before hugging Alexander.

Once he released me, I turned toward Lachlan, who squeezed me tightly, leaving a tender kiss on my temple.

"Take care of yourself, kid."

I rolled my eyes, feigning annoyance at the nickname he gave me when he started dating my mom all those years ago. Even though I was now in my thirties, I wouldn't want him to call me anything else.

"Of course."

"I'll miss you, sweetie," Mama said, wrapping her arms around me. "But I'm happy for you." She pulled back, holding my biceps. "California looks good on you." She lowered her voice. "Or maybe it's a certain *someone* who looks good on you."

"Maybe it's both."

"You deserve it. And don't let anyone else make you think otherwise." She gave me a knowing look.

"I won't."

"Speaking of which..." She nodded toward the lobby doors as Gideon entered, looking absolutely sinful in his linen shirt and jeans. Then again, he could probably make a paper sack look good. "Looks like your ride's here."

I bit my lower lip, trying to reel in the butterflies swimming in my stomach as he walked toward me with a confident stride, touching a soft kiss to my cheek.

It was incredibly freeing to allow another man to kiss me in public. For years, I'd avoided it because of Liam.

No more.

"Ready?" Gideon asked, his warm hand brushing against my arm.

I nodded. "Thanks for taking me to the airport."

"Anything to spend more time with you," he replied with a disarming smile.

I said another round of goodbyes to everyone, promising to call Melanie when I landed. Then Gideon guided me out of the lobby, pulling my luggage behind him.

"I still can't believe you drove all the way here," I remarked as he navigated his gorgeous Jaguar convertible along the 17 Mile Drive. "I guess if I had a car like this, I'd probably drive, too." I ran my hand along the dashboard, everything smooth and pristine.

"Need me to give you and the car a moment alone?"

"Very funny." I tilted my head back, savoring in the feel of the sun on my face. "It's the perfect driving weather. Not too hot. Not too cold. Especially along the coast."

"Why don't you come with me?"

I darted my gaze toward him. "What?"

"We're going to the same place. May as well go together." He stole a glance at me, dragging a finger up my inner thigh. "I promise to make it much more...enjoyable than flying all day. And don't you have a connection up in San Francisco, anyway?"

"Yes," I groaned.

I *was* supposed to fly back with Liam on his jet, but after last night, I thought it best if I found my own way to San Diego. Unfortunately, since I was booking at the last minute, the best flight I could get included a three-hour layover.

"Then come with me." He extended his hand toward me in anticipation. "Let's have an adventure."

I sucked in a sudden intake of air, momentarily speechless.

That was what Samuel always said before we were about to do something together. It didn't even have to be anything big or dangerous. With Samuel, *everything* was an adventure, even something as mundane as cooking dinner.

I raked my gaze over Gideon's silhouette. Nothing about it remotely resembled Samuel. Gideon's jaw was more square, his nose a tad crooked, his cheekbones higher and more pronounced. He *wasn't* Samuel.

Just because he said something that reminded me of him didn't mean anything. I needed to stop sabotaging what could be a good thing by clinging to a ghost.

"Let's have an adventure," I repeated, placing my hand in his.

And that was where it stayed for most of the day as we embarked on our first adventure together.

Hopefully, it would be the first of many.

CHAPTER THIRTY-ONE

Gideon

"What's the status?" I asked as I stepped into my office early Monday morning after spending the night at Imogene's townhouse.

I hated having to leave her, would have loved to stay wrapped in her arms all day. What made it even worse was waking up to Ollie jumping on us, much like he did all those years ago.

But I needed to get home. Needed to prepare for what today would bring. I couldn't afford to get distracted, not when I was this close. Which was why I told Imogene I'd be heading out of town on business for a few days.

It wasn't a complete lie. At some point this week, I *would* be heading out of town.

But it wasn't on business, at least not in the way she thought.

Instead, it would be to kill Alton. To finally vindicate the part he played in my demise, as well as Jonah's death.

"Look who decided to join the party," Henry retorted.

I ignored him, striding purposefully toward the rows of camera feeds displayed on the various screens throughout the room. Each one showed a different part of Alton's life — his corner office overlooking Central Park in New York, his sleek office in Los Angeles, his luxurious homes scattered across the country.

Henry even managed to install cameras in a hunting cabin he owned in the mountains not many people knew about. Which was where I had a feeling he planned to hide out once everything unraveled in the coming days.

"What's he been doing?" I pressed.

"He had a cleaning crew come into his LA office yesterday. Same with New York."

"And by cleaning crew..."

"I'm not talking about people who scrub the toilets and vacuum the carpet."

"So they were shredding documents."

He nodded. "Looks like Alton's worried what the feds might find should they investigate his latest blunder. Which they will, thanks to a tip from a whistleblower on the inside." He winked.

"What about James and Liam?"

"They're not answering his calls."

"Damn."

"James can't have any appearance of impropriety, considering his position in the government, so he's distanced himself."

"He'll get what's coming to him soon enough," I assured him.

"As for Liam..."

"Liam's just an asshole who disposes of people when they no longer have any use to him," I finished.

"That about sums it up. Plus, he has bigger concerns with the body that was found on his boat."

"Did the police pull the surveillance video from the marina?"

"Sure did." Henry flashed that conniving grin of his. "Pity to find the hard drive was corrupted."

"Gee, I wonder how that happened," I remarked sarcastically.

"It's a mystery, one even the best tech geniuses will never be able to solve. Of course, considering Liam's background in computers, the police are even more suspicious of him now."

I chuckled. "Remind me to never get on your bad side."

"Likewise."

I gave his shoulder a squeeze, then turned from him, heading out of the office.

"Where are you going?" Henry asked.

"To get some rest."

"You don't want to watch it all fall apart?" He nodded at the clock on the wall that showed it was mere minutes before 6:30. The stock market would open soon, and when it did, GeoCom's stock would most likely take a giant nosedive off a cliff.

I glanced at the feed of Alton's Los Angeles office where he currently sat on the edge of his couch, his leg nervously bouncing as his anxious stare remained fixed on the large television on the opposite wall. A stock ticker scrolled along the bottom of the screen as a reporter discussed the legal trouble GeoCom's CEO was in and what it meant for the company going forward.

The prognosis wasn't good.

"I'd rather be well rested so nothing goes wrong when it really matters."

"And you're sure that's still what you want?" He arched a brow.

"Why wouldn't it be?"

"Just making sure. It's still not too late to walk away. Once you take this next step, there's no going back. There's no choice but to follow through to the end." He narrowed his gaze at me. "But right now, you *still* have that choice."

I stared into the distance, ruminating his words over in my mind.

Did I have a choice?

Could I forget this entire thing and stop living in the past?

I would have been lying if I said I hadn't thought about that more and more the past few days, especially as I spent time with Imogene.

As I made love to her.

As she ran her fingers over each of my scars and called them beautiful.

It was so tempting.

But I wasn't only doing this for myself.

I was doing this for Jonah.

For his mother.

"There *is* no choice," I told Henry in a determined voice. "To the end. No going back."

He pushed out a long sigh. "No going back."

CHAPTER THIRTY-TWO

Gideon

Darkness surrounded me as I crouched amongst towering redwood and sequoia trees. The only light came from the tiny sliver of a moon and the thousands of stars scattered across the sky. They seemed even brighter tonight, especially out here in the middle of nowhere, no light pollution to dull their vibrancy.

At one point in my life, I never understood why someone would want to live this far removed from civilization. Now, it sounded like the perfect place to end my time on earth.

Just like Alton was about to.

As was predicted, when the markets opened Monday morning, GeoCom stock tanked. Within hours of the opening bell, their board unanimously voted to temporarily remove the CEO, pending an official investigation into the allegations against him.

That did little to restore confidence in the market, considering there was evidence of a company-wide culture of sexual abuse, as well as bribing victims and law enforcement to keep it quiet. Instead of the stock price recovering with a new interim CEO, it kept falling over the course of the past several days as more evidence came to light.

It appeared that would continue for the foreseeable future.

To make matters worse, investigators learned that, not only was Alton involved in insider trading, but he'd also been lying to his clients. Made them believe their investments were safe with him. All along, Alton was pocketing huge sums of their money to finance his lavish lifestyle.

He'd stolen dozens of people's life savings.

Further proof he only cared about himself.

And money.

"I've remotely disabled his security system," Henry's voice sounded over the small earpiece I wore. "You probably have about an hour to get in, get it done, and get out before the FBI comes knocking, thanks to a little anonymous tip."

While Alton may have done everything to make it so no one could trace this particular property back to him, going so far as paying cash for it and buying it in the name of a shell corporation, I needed the authorities to find his body. Needed them to comb his property for evidence.

Needed to give Liam and James yet another reason to shit their pants.

"You ready?"

"I've been preparing for this day for five years," I responded in a low voice. "I'll check in when it's done."

With slow, deliberate movements, I rose from my hiding spot in the dense woods surrounding the simple log cabin. Every step I took was calculated, each footfall carefully placed as to make as little noise as possible, each crunch of my boots against the leaves and sticks amplified.

When I reached the back door, I paused, my fingers hovering over the keypad.

This was it — the point of no return. Once I walked into this house and killed Alton, there would be no turning back. It would set everything else into motion.

But it wasn't too late yet.

I could still back out.

I already had Imogene, in a way. Wasn't that enough?

I wanted it to be. There was a time I might have been happy with that.

That was before I truly understood what these men I once considered friends had done.

All to pad their pockets.

I couldn't let them get away with it any longer.

They needed to learn exactly what it felt like to lose everything. To feel powerless as their world crumbled around them.

To stare into my eyes as they realized who was behind their demise.

Just as I did.

Pushing down any lingering doubts, I punched the unlock code Henry had given me into the pad. When it beeped, I quietly opened the door and slipped into the darkened kitchen. I removed my gun from its holster, keeping it raised, just in case.

"He's in the study. Front left of the house," Henry instructed through my earpiece.

I nodded, silently moving through the kitchen and into the living area, pausing outside a wooden door that was slightly ajar.

Closing my eyes, I took a steadying breath, steeling myself for what I was about to do. There was once a time when I couldn't fathom the idea of taking another man's life.

That was before I had no choice but to kill or be killed. Alton's actions had turned me into a killer.

It was time he suffered the consequences.

Touching my hand against the wood, I pushed the door open and stepped into the study.

A loud, unexpected creak reverberated through the dimly lit room, causing Alton to startle from his place on the leather couch. He straightened, fumbling for the gun he'd carelessly left abandoned on the coffee table.

Unfortunately for him, the scotch he'd consumed throughout the day left his reflexes slow, allowing me to grab the weapon with my gloved hand before he could.

"Nice try," I said, shoving his gun into the back of my pants as I kept my weapon trained on him. "Here's a tip. If you're worried someone might find you after you cost them their life's savings, it's probably best you *not* drink yourself into a stupor."

"Gideon."

He swallowed hard, his normally red face becoming ashen, his chin trembling. Beads of sweat formed on his lip and forehead, his eyes focused on the gun in my hand.

I knew exactly how he felt. It was how I felt when I saw the man I trusted more than anyone point a gun at me.

Except he didn't give me an explanation. Didn't give me a chance to stop him. Instead, he pulled the trigger and left me for dead.

"Is that why you're here?"

His quivering voice lacked all the bravado it did this

past weekend when he was hitting on every woman with a pulse as if it were his right.

"If that's the case, I don't—"

I threw my head back and laughed. "The money I invested with you is peanuts to me. I understand the unpredictable nature of the market. There are ups and downs." I pinched my lips together. "Of course, I'd prefer the downs not be because my portfolio manager traded on bad information."

"Then..."

"You were right." I lowered myself into the leather chair opposite him.

"I was?"

"Yes." I gestured to the crystal bottle on the coffee table. "Do you mind?"

He gave a confused nod. I doubted he'd tell me no, considering I currently had a gun pointed directly at him.

"I *did* plan this," I explained as I poured some scotch into a rocks glass. But instead of taking a sip, I simply swirled the amber liquid around, watching it dance and sparkle in the light.

"I purposefully left the draft press release out for you to see, knowing you wouldn't be able to resist the temptation." I hesitated. "At least I *hoped* you wouldn't. Hoped things hadn't changed that much in the past five years." A small smirk tugged at the corner of my lips. "Luckily, they hadn't. You still can't resist the allure of using inside information to your advantage just to add a few zeroes to your bank account."

"I..." He licked his lips, the trembles in his body becoming more pronounced. "I don't know what you're talking about."

"It's the same reason you agreed to Liam's plan to kill Samuel and frame Jonah for it, isn't it? Even made a statement that you remembered seeing the weapon allegedly used to kill him in Jonah's backpack."

"I don't—"

"Oh, come on, Alton. No need to lie now. I know everything. I know how Liam told you all about Image-Scape's offer to buy Cloud Hero for quite a pretty penny, which would certainly increase their stock. So you went all in on ImageScape, didn't you? Bought up as many shares as you could. Just like you did last week with GeoCom. But neither of you expected that Samuel wouldn't want to sell out. You couldn't understand why he wouldn't accept an offer that would make him a billionaire. And you certainly didn't expect he'd want to go in the opposite direction, turn Cloud Hero into an employee-owned company."

The more I spoke, the more uneasy Alton became, his expression growing paler by the second.

"And you couldn't have that, could you? You both stood to make a fortune — Liam by selling, and you by the increased value of all the ImageScape stocks you'd already bought, which would allow you to pay dividends to some of your investors so they wouldn't get suspicious you'd been stealing from them. So you agreed to kill him and cover it up."

"I..." He shook his head. "We had nothing to do with that. Some loser kid did it."

I shot to my feet and rushed toward him, shoving my gun against his temple. "Loser kid?" I seethed, unable to control my anger. "Let me tell you something about Jonah Pruitt. He had more integrity in his pinky finger than you have in your entire body. He was someone who was willing to stand up for what was right, regardless of what might happen to him." My voice thundered through the room, the windows seeming to rattle with my fury. "He was trying to break the cycle. Hoped to go to college and become a computer engineer. But you assholes pinned a murder on him instead. Then you made sure he was dead before he could prove his innocence."

"I..."

"Tell me I'm wrong!" I roared, my finger tightening on the trigger. "Go ahead, Alton. Lie, and see what happens."

"H-how did you know Jonah?" he asked after several long moments. "Were you friends with Samuel?"

I brought my face within an inch of his, wanting to look into his eyes when he learned the truth.

"No, Alton. I *am* Samuel."

Any remaining color in his face instantly drained, his breaths bursting in and out.

"You can't be. It's not possible. You're dead."

"They never found my body. Did they?"

"But the blood. They said—"

"That no one could have survived that kind of wound." I straightened, pacing in front of him. "You're right. I *shouldn't* have survived. But someone found me. Patched me up. Unfortunately, he wasn't the good Samaritan I thought he was. Instead, he took me to what I can only describe as a living hell where I had to either kill or be killed. I'll let you guess which I chose."

"Please, Sammy."

"Don't you dare call me that," I hissed, pointing my weapon at him once more. "I'm not Sammy. Hell, I'm not even Samuel. Not anymore. Samuel died in that car. Just like you all planned."

"We used to be friends. This isn't you. You're not a killer."

"That's where you're wrong, Alton." I leaned into him, my face mere inches from his. "I *am* a killer. You turned me into one. And it's time you pay for what you've done. Not just to me. But to Jonah."

Setting my gun onto the coffee table, I retrieved his

weapon and forced him to hold it against his head, carefully adjusting the angle so the wound would appear self-inflicted. I was fully prepared to use one of the guns I'd brought, but using his makes it even cleaner.

"Please," he whimpered again, a wet stain covering his crotch, the acrid stench of piss filling the room. "I don't want to die."

"You should have thought about that before you agreed to kill me." When I added pressure to the trigger, Alton's entire body trembled as he pleaded for his life.

I was surprised he didn't try to fight me. Not like he'd win. Still, I expected some pushback. Instead, he just continued to sob and beg for forgiveness until a blast echoed in the room, leaving behind a splatter of blood and tissue on the opposite wall.

I carefully released my hold on his hand and allowed his arm to fall limply beside his body, ensuring it still held the gun. Then I stood and removed a glove, bringing the glass of scotch I'd poured earlier up to my mouth.

I downed it in several long swallows, a weight lifting off my shoulders as I took a final look at the gaping hole in Alton's head.

One down. Two to go.

CHAPTER THIRTY-THREE

Imogene

The sound of a gentle rapping cut through a dreamless sleep, and I bolted upright, still slightly disoriented from being woken so abruptly. If it weren't for Ollie's barking, I would have thought I'd imagined the noise.

Rubbing my eyes, I tapped the screen on my phone to see it was a little after two in the morning. Who could be knocking on my door this late?

Maybe it was Liam. He'd had a rough few days with both the cops questioning him about Benjamin Astor and the GeoCom stock tanking. It wouldn't surprise me to learn he'd gotten drunk and decided now was a good time to talk, even if we hadn't spoken since our argument in Pebble Beach.

But when I checked my doorbell app and saw Gideon standing on my porch, I sprang out of bed, my feet pounding down the stairs and into the living room, flinging the door open.

"Gideon," I exhaled breathlessly. "Is everything okay?"

He parted his lips to respond, then snapped them shut, his eyes focused on my chest.

As I glanced at the t-shirt covering my body, the logo for the teen program Samuel founded prominent, along with his name, I realized what caught his attention.

After he died, I'd taken this t-shirt from his things. Wore it practically every hour of the day. As time went on, I eventually wore it less and less, typically just to bed. It didn't even faze me when I threw it on last night. And I just answered the door for new man in my life while wearing my dead boyfriend's t-shirt.

In my defense, I hadn't expected to see Gideon. He told me he'd be out of town until tomorrow at the earliest.

"Sorry. It's a habit. I usually wear this to bed. I didn't even think—"

Before I could utter another syllable, Gideon crushed his mouth to mine, pushing me into my house without invitation.

He didn't need one, though. I didn't care why he knocked on my door in the middle of the night. Nothing mattered other than the warmth of his lips against mine, his greedy fingers digging into my skin.

It had only been four days since I'd tasted him, but after spending every possible minute with him last weekend, those four days may as well have been four years for how much I craved him.

When he finally tore away, I panted, struggling to catch my breath.

"Don't ever apologize for your past, Imogene." He tightened his grip on my cheeks, not allowing me to escape. "It made you who you are. Just like each one of my scars made me who *I* am. So don't apologize for who you are." His lips slowly descended toward mine. "Because I'll tell you a secret."

"What's that?"

"I'm starting to fall for you. Exactly as you are now."

Hooking my arm around his shoulders, I hoisted myself onto my toes and brushed my lips against his.

Was it crazy to feel this way? Were we setting ourselves up for failure by moving too fast? We'd only known each other a few weeks. How well could anyone really know someone in such a short amount of time?

But then I thought about my mama and Lachlan. They knew after spending even less time together and were still happily married over fifteen years later. Mama always said the universe gave her precisely what she needed in Lachlan.

Maybe the universe had given me precisely what *I* needed in Gideon.

"And I'm starting to fall for you," I finally admitted, my throat welling with emotion. "Exactly as you are now."

He covered my mouth with his as his hands roamed my frame. When they skimmed my ass, only to find me bare, he groaned. In one swift motion, he lifted me up, my legs instinctively wrapping around his waist as he carried me up the stairs.

Once we reached my bedroom, he carefully placed me onto my mattress. Straightening, he took his time to remove his hoodie and t-shirt, revealing the intricate patterns of scars that adorned his torso.

I'd never been so drawn to the sight of another man stripping before. With Gideon, it was different. I knew what a big deal it was for him to let me see this side of him. To see each and every scar that marred his body. But I meant what I told him.

They *were* beautiful.

I'd forever be grateful he trusted me enough with this part of him. With his past.

Like I'd finally trusted him with *my* past.

His wanton stare heated my flesh as he pushed his jeans down his legs and tossed them to the side. Crawling on top of me, he captured my mouth with his, his body moving sensually against mine.

"I need to feel you," he begged, gently pulsing against me. "Nothing between us."

I scraped my nails up and down his back, his hard erection against my center driving me wild with need.

I'd certainly imagined how he'd feel inside me, flesh to flesh, even if a part of me resisted the idea. The last person who'd been inside of me without a condom was Samuel.

But I needed this. Needed to feel him. I no longer wanted anything standing between us. Not my past. Not *his* past. Instead, it would just be us and this intense connection I felt from the first time I stared into his eyes.

Arching toward him, I took his earlobe between my teeth. "Let me feel you, Gideon."

He cupped my cheeks, his eyes boring into mine. Then his lips collided with mine in a fierce kiss as he eased inside me, everything about it new and invigorating.

And not because this was the first time he hadn't worn a condom.

Instead, as he brought me to the brink of orgasm, only to retreat, dragging out my bliss, this was so much more than just sex.

It was relief.

It was deliverance.

It was salvation.

The way he held my face as he moved inside of me

made me feel like he was able to peer directly into my soul.

It was too much, yet not enough. I wanted more of him. Wanted all of him. Wanted every one of his broken, shattered pieces so I could be the glue to put them back together.

Just like this man had become *my* glue, even when I didn't want to admit it. Even when I was still clinging to the past.

As our bodies moved in time with each other, there were no lust-filled declarations. No wanton orders. No needy remarks.

Instead, I stayed in the moment with Gideon, neither one of us looking away for so much as a heartbeat. We didn't even need to tell each other when we were getting close. We just knew, our bodies singing a song only we could hear until we had nothing left to give and fell asleep wrapped up in each other.

CHAPTER THIRTY-FOUR

Imogene

A sliver of sunlight peeked through the curtains, causing me to flutter my eyes open and take in the disarray that was my bedroom. And not simply because of the piles of unpacked boxes that were still stacked against nearly every wall.

But because of all the clothes and blankets scattered about, the result of Gideon's and my ravenous appetite for each other. The man was insatiable, more so than ever. For the first time since we started sleeping together, he didn't hold back. Like whatever had been burdening him had been lifted.

Sensing me stir beside him, he pulled me closer and pressed his hips against mine, his erection prominent.

"You're an animal," I said, my voice raspy from lack of sleep.

"I won't apologize for being ridiculously attracted to you." He ran his hand along my stomach, inching lower and lower.

I parted my thighs, giving him better access. When his thumb and forefinger lightly pinched my clit, I closed my eyes and released a moan.

"Seems you're just as desperate for me as I am for you." He scraped his unshaven jawline against my neck.

"Always," I exhaled, moving in time with his ministrations.

He slipped a finger inside of me before adding another.

"So warm," he crooned, circling his hips against me. "So wet." He curved toward me, nipping at my skin.

I had a feeling it was currently riddled with small marks from all the times he'd bitten me last night, but I didn't mind. I would happily wear the proof of Gideon's unyielding hunger for me.

"So mine."

"Yours," I whimpered as he lined himself up at my entrance, about to thrust inside.

Unfortunately, that was the precise moment Ollie decided to jump onto the bed, showering both of us with kisses.

"Cockblocker," Gideon laughed, scratching Ollie's head.

"I think someone wants to go out." I glanced at my phone to see it was already after six. "He's used to getting up early."

"I can take him for a walk. That way, you can get ready for work."

I rolled over to face him, which prompted Ollie to bestow me with even more kisses. I tried to swat him away, but there was no coming between my dog and the prospect of chasing birds on the beach.

"Are you sure you don't mind?"

"Of course not." He smoothed a few tendrils of hair behind my ear. "Plus, it'll give us some time to get to know each other so he can hopefully give me the stamp of approval." Leaving a kiss on my forehead, he climbed out of bed. Ollie bounded off the mattress, as well, following him every step of the way.

"Stamp of approval?" I rolled onto my side and watched him pull on his jeans, propping my head in my hand. "For what?"

"To continue spending time with you. If you ask me, getting your dog's stamp of approval is much more important than getting your best friend's. Or even your parents'. Humans can be fooled easily. Not dogs."

"True. But I'll let you in on a little secret."

"What's that?" He tugged on his shirt, then zipped up his hoodie.

"Ollie's a complete sucker for the pup cups at The Daily Grind. Get him one of those, and you'll be on his good list forever."

"Duly noted." He touched his lips to mine before turning and slipping out of the room, whistling for Ollie to follow.

And for the first time, I didn't allow the fact that Samuel once whistled for him just like that to cloud my rationale. Instead, I dragged myself out of bed and into the shower, the only thought on my mind that of the feel of Gideon thrusting inside of me.

I'd love nothing more than to stay in bed all day with him as we pretended the world didn't exist. It was crazy to think that this time last week, I purposefully avoided going anywhere I might run into him.

Now, I'd give anything to see him every second of the day.

I may not have known a lot about him, but I did know I liked how he made me feel. Liked that he didn't try to shame me for anything. Didn't try to make me feel guilty for things outside of my control.

For now, that was enough.

Hell, that was *everything*.

After showering and styling my hair in a loose braid, I made my way down to the kitchen just as Gideon opened the front door, Ollie bounding inside, his tongue hanging from his mouth.

"Sorry we're just getting back now," Gideon said, unhooking Ollie's leash and draping it over the hook in the foyer. It was so domesticated. As if this place was as much his as it was mine.

As if he'd always been a part of my life.

"Your dog's a complete chick magnet. Everyone at The Daily Grind loves him." He set a tray containing two coffee cups and a paper bag onto the kitchen table.

"He's a dick magnet, too."

A low growl echoed, but not from Ollie.

"I'm not sure I like the sound of that."

"Don't worry." I scooped some kibble into Ollie's bowl. He didn't waste any time in barreling toward it and chowing down on his breakfast. "Ollie's extremely protective of me. Usually growls at anyone with a penis who tries to get too close." I laughed under my breath. "Pretty sure his dad taught him..." I trailed off. "Sorry. I'm doing it again."

"Imogene..." Gideon approached me, cupping my face in his strong hands. "I meant what I said last night. Your past is a part of you. Don't hide it from me. If talking about him makes you feel better, I'll listen. Okay?"

I drew in a deep breath, then nodded.

"Good." He covered my lips with his, then pushed

out a frustrated sigh. "As much as I don't want to, I have some work to catch up on. Can I call you later?"

"Sure."

He smiled, then scrunched his brows. "I don't think I even have your phone number."

I opened my mouth to argue, but snapped it shut when I realized he was right. We may have had sex more times than I could count. At least more times than I'd had in the past five years. But I didn't know his phone number.

"How is that possible?"

"I have no idea," he chuckled, passing me his cell. "Add your contact info."

After typing in my name and number, I handed it back. A smirk curved on his mouth as his fingers flew over the screen.

Seconds later, my phone buzzed in my pocket and I retrieved it.

GIDEON:

Whenever you miss me during the day,
think of how good you take my cock.

Biting back my infectious grin, I typed out a response and hit send.

ME:

> But that will only make me miss you more. And it might make me want to touch myself, which I know is against the rules. So I may just need to be punished.

When he checked his phone, his jaw ticked as his dark gaze met mine.

With slow steps, he moved toward me, wrapping his fingers around my throat. "I believe that can be arranged, Ms. Prescott."

I peered up at him with wide, doe eyes. "I'm looking forward to it, Mr. Saint."

CHAPTER THIRTY-FIVE

Imogene

I didn't think today was ever going to end. Not because I didn't love my job.

But because of all the texts Gideon kept sending, each one becoming increasingly explicit, turning me on more and more.

Which was incredibly inconvenient, since I was at work and couldn't do anything about the ache between my legs.

It got so bad that I told him I was turning off my phone and would text him when I was off work.

So he could hopefully get *me* off.

I just prayed he would be able to come over. I was desperate to see him. Not just to have sex, although that certainly entered into the equation.

But because I genuinely enjoyed his company. I loved how he accepted me as I was, quirks and all.

Loved how good he was to Ollie, something Liam never was.

Loved how we could sit in silence and it not feel awkward, like during our road trip down the coast.

The more time I spent with him, the more I believed some higher power sent him my way to help heal the hole in my heart left behind by Samuel's absence.

Better yet, maybe Samuel sent him to tell me it was okay to move on.

Approaching my car, I hit the unlock button on my key fob and opened the door. My bag landed on the passenger's seat with a thump as I climbed behind the wheel, pulling out my cell and powering it on.

As expected, I was bombarded with multiple texts.

But they weren't from Gideon.

Instead, they were from Melanie, my parents, and even Liam.

But that wasn't all.

A breaking news alert flashed across the screen, announcing that Alton Sinclair had been found in a remote mountain cabin, dead from an apparent suicide.

Regret squeezed at my chest as I recalled some of the things I'd said about him.

I was never particularly close to him. I always found him somewhat egotistical and pompous. Not to mention,

I hated how he treated women and definitely didn't approve of his business practices that had come to light in recent days.

Regardless of my personal feelings toward him, I still didn't wish death on him.

I quickly hit Melanie's contact as I put my car into drive, my mind spinning.

"Gin!" Melanie exhaled, relief filling her voice. "I was so worried. Your phone was going straight to voice-mail, and after..." She trailed off, her words catching. "Well, I'm glad you're okay. Did you hear about Alton?"

"I did," I replied in a shaky voice. "I'm sorry. I didn't mean to worry you."

"I knew you were at work, but after everything." She fought to reel in her emotions. "I didn't even like that asshole, but I can't believe he's—"

"I know." I swallowed hard. "Have you spoken with Liam?"

"A few hours ago."

"How is he?"

"I don't know. He sounded...off."

"Off?" I echoed.

"I don't know how to explain it. I'm heading down right now to see him. Will you be there?" she asked hesitantly, fully aware of the argument we got into a few days ago.

Now I felt even worse about that argument.

What if I'd turned on my phone and learned Liam had died?

I'd never forgive myself for the way I treated him. We may have had our disagreements, but I wasn't completely heartless. I still cared about him.

"I'll be there," I assured her.

"Good. See you soon. Drive carefully."

"You, too."

"And Imogene?"

"Yeah?"

"I love you."

"I love you, too, Mel."

I ended the call, then tossed my cell onto the front seat, sending up a silent prayer for Alton.

I'd never been one to pray, but it felt like the right thing to do. Plus, what else was I going to do while I inched along the freeway?

After a longer than normal drive through heavy traffic, I finally pulled up to the ornate gate at the entrance to Liam's house and punched in my access code. I half expected it wouldn't work. Thankfully, the gate sprung open and I navigated my car up the cobbled drive, parking in front of his home.

"Ms. Prescott," Liam's housekeeper greeted when she answered the door.

"I'm sorry for showing up like this, but is Liam— Mr.

Pierce here? I just heard the news and wanted to check on him."

She gave me a sympathetic smile. "Of course, dear. He's in his office with Senator Turner. I'm sure he'll be happy to see you, though. They both will."

"Thank you."

I stepped into the cavernous entryway, my footfalls echoing against the polished marble tile.

As I walked down the darkened hallway toward his office, a heavy sense of unease settled over me. I tried to brush it off, tell myself it was natural for there to be an ominous feeling in the air. Alton had just killed himself, for crying out loud.

But as I drew closer to Liam's office, the feeling intensified, sending a chill down my spine.

I paused outside the door and drew in a deep breath before reaching out to knock. When I heard raised voices coming from inside, I hesitated, straining to listen.

"Maybe it's an old glass," Liam said, his tone laced with anxiety. "One that hasn't been washed lately."

"One that was conveniently left on the coffee table next to Alton's?" James countered, his voice mirroring the nerves in Liam's.

"What other possible explanation is there?" Liam interjected, his frustration increasing by the second.

I imagined him pacing the length of the room as he

tugged on his hair. Or tie. Or guzzled whatever he was drinking.

It was more than apparent something had him on edge. Something to do with a glass. But *what* glass? And why was that important? Did they find something indicating that perhaps Alton *didn't* kill himself?

"Somebody must have made a mistake," Liam continued, as if his declaration would make it so. "Have them run the prints again."

"They already have. *Twice.* Along with quite a few other items found in close proximity to Alton's body. Initially, it was to confirm the cause of death, but the second glass on the coffee table stumped them, so they ran it to see if someone else was in the room with Alton." He lowered his voice. "To see if maybe *you* were in the room with him, considering...recent events."

"I told you!" Liam roared. "I have no idea how that damn body ended up on my boat. I haven't been to that marina in months. There's no record of me using my access card at the gate."

"I believe you, but that doesn't change the evidence they uncovered at Alton's cabin."

No one spoke for several long moments, the only sound that of a grandfather clock keeping time in the distance.

"What does this mean?" Liam asked finally.

"Either someone planted his fingerprints there to fuck with us."

"Or..." Liam prodded, although I could hear the hesitation in his voice.

"Or Samuel Tate's back from the dead."

Thank you for reading *Cruel Saint*! I hope you enjoyed the first part of Gideon and Imogene's story. Will Imogene finally uncover the truth? Find out today.

https://getbook.at/TemptingDevil

Thanks again for taking the time to read this book. If you enjoyed it, please let your friends know by leaving a review so more people can fall in love with Gideon and Imogene.

TEMPTING DEVIL

After five years, I'm finally about to get everything I've dreamed of — revenge against the men who destroyed my life.

There's just one tiny complication — Imogene Prescott.

She was just supposed to be a tool, someone I'd use then toss out with the trash I thought she was.

She wasn't supposed to get under my skin.

She wasn't supposed to give me a reason to live.

But she did.

Now I have a choice to make — love or revenge.

But no matter what I chose, I fear it won't be enough to protect her from the dangerous truth I've hidden from her.

Confucius warned to dig two graves when embarking on a journey of revenge.

I didn't plan on one of those graves belonging to her.

Scan below or type the address into your web browser.

https://getbook.at/TemptingDevil

ACKNOWELDGMENTS

Ever since I first started this author journey over ten years ago, I'd always wanted to write a retelling of one of my favorite stories — *The Count of Monte Cristo*. There's just something about a good revenge trope I absolutely love. So this story has been simmering in the back of my mind for over ten years now. Unfortunately, I just didn't have the right characters to pull it off... Until now.

When I teased Imogene's story at the end of my Temptation Series, I knew I'd finally found the character who would be perfect for this retelling. It's certainly been quite the ride... And it's just beginning. I can't wait for you to see what I have in store for the next two books in this trilogy.

But first, there are a few people I need to acknowledge for all their help.

First and foremost, a huge thanks to my husband,

Stan, and my daughter, Harper Leigh. I couldn't do this without their support.

To my wonderful PA, Melissa Crump — I'd be lost without you. Thanks for all your love and support.

To my fantastic beta readers — Lin, Melissa, Sylvia, Stacy, and Vicky — thanks for always reading for me and offering feedback.

To my admin team — Melissa and Vicky. Thanks for keeping my reader group and page running. Love you ladies!

To my review team — Thank you for always not only reading my books but also taking the time to write reviews. Your support means the world to me.

To my reader group — Thanks for being my super-fans and giving me a place to go when I need a break from writing.

And last but not least, a big thank you to YOU! My amazing readers. I'm so grateful for your support. Whether this was your first book or mine or your thirty-first, I'm truly grateful for your support.

Can't wait to share the next chapter of Imogene and Gideon's story with you.

Love & Peace,

~ T.K.

ABOUT THE AUTHOR

T.K. Leigh is a *USA Today* Bestselling author of romance ranging from fun and flirty to sexy and suspenseful.

Originally from New England, she now resides just outside of Raleigh with her husband, beautiful daughter, rescued special needs dog, and three cats. When she's not writing, she can be found training for her next marathon or chasing her daughter around the house.

facebook.com/tkleighauthor

instagram.com/tkleigh

tiktok.com/@tkleigh

bookbub.com/authors/t-k-leigh

pinterest.com/tkleighauthor